A Village Romeo and Juliet

Gottfried Keller

Translated by Ronald Taylor

WITHDRAWN
UTSA Libraries

ONEWORLD
CLASSICS

ONEWORLD CLASSICS
243-253 Lower Mortlake Road
Richmond
Surrey TW9 2LL
United Kingdom
www.oneworldclassics.com

A Village Romeo and Juliet first published in German in 1856

First published in this translation in 1966 by John Calder (Publishers) Limited
Translation © John Calder (Publishers) Limited, 1966
This edition first published by Oneworld Classics Limited in 2008

Typeset by Alma Books Ltd

Front cover image © Getty Images

Printed in Great Britain by Intypelibra, Wimbledon

ISBN: 978-1-84749-086-5

All rights reserved. No part of this publication may be reproduced, stored in or introduced into a retrieval system, or transmitted, in any form or by any means (electronic, mechanical, photocopying, recording or otherwise), without the prior written permission of the publisher. This book is sold subject to the condition that it shall not be resold, lent, hired out or otherwise circulated without the express prior consent of the publisher.

Library
University of Texas
at San Antonio

Contents

Introduction

G OTTFRIED KELLER, one of the greatest narrative writers of German literature, was born in Zürich in 1819. His family was poor and his education rudimentary, and after leaving school at fifteen he took up the study of painting, first in Zürich, then in Munich. But his faith in his artistic calling was not matched by his talent, and after two years in Munich he returned to his native town.

Turning his mind to writing instead of painting, he succeeded in having a group of poems published in a literary magazine, and on the basis of the promise which these poems revealed, he received a grant from the government of his canton to study at a university abroad. With this he went to Heidelberg, where he came under the strong influence of the materialist philosopher Feuerbach. After two years he left for Berlin, where he stayed from 1850 to 1855, publishing a further volume of poems and completing his first and most important novel, the autobiographical romance *Der grüne Heinrich.* Immediately after this he began to work at great speed on the succession of short stories by which he is best known today: those collected into two volumes under the title *Die Leute von Seldwyla.*

In 1855 Keller returned to Switzerland, and in 1861 was offered a position in the cantonal administration of Zürich. This post he held for fifteen years, during which time he published his *Sieben Legenden* and the cycle of historical stories *Zürcher Novellen.* He died in Zürich in 1890, four days before his seventy-first birthday.

It is in his shorter narrative works that Keller is seen at his strongest and most gripping. His subject matter is often of slender proportions, and its setting provincial, but the pitiless penetration of his gaze and the blunt insistence of his manner – he was no respecter of persons – create from it works of ruthless characterization and rugged situational power. He is no polished stylist, like his contemporary and countryman Conrad Ferdinand Meyer; indeed, his descriptive writing is often repetitious and technically inept, and one must sometimes wonder that it does not seriously detract from the effectiveness of the finished product. Yet the forceful realism of that product remains unshakeable – a blend of his observed experience of the people about whom he wrote and his relentless pursuit of significant detail.

The genesis of *Romeo und Julia auf dem Dorfe* lies in a Zürich newspaper report of the suicide of two young lovers who have been driven to desperation by the antagonism between their two families. Keller read this report at the time and sought to provide from his imagination a series of circumstances that could have led to a family feud; and the circumstances that he created were made to bear the motivation both of the degradation of the rival families and the ultimate tragedy of the lovers.

But for all his eloquent presentation of their imagined love, Keller has concerns that go beyond the personal fate of Sali and Vrenchen, for these two unhappy creatures are but the helpless victims of forces that issue from the evil ways of others; and these others, moreover, are Keller's fellow citizens from the locality of his symbolical town of Seldwyla. The malice and intolerance of the fathers; the thinly veiled hostility of most of the onlookers; jealousy that so complete and pure a love should be vouchsafed to, of all people, the children of such despicable families; and the Black Fiddler's devilish attempts to seduce the lovers into exchanging a life of light-hearted abandon in his kingdom of immoral freedom for their doomed existence among the cruelties of a so-called moral society: these are the malevolent realities that condition the lives of Vrenchen and Sali. And there is no simple, benevolent deity who can be called upon to officiate at the restoration of simple, benevolent, optimistic faith. It is characteristic of Keller's forthrightness that this situation is left – and resolved – in the realistic, uncompromising terms that express his own view of life and human fate.

R.T.

Chronology

1819   Born in Zürich on 19th July.

1834   Expelled from school and took up the study of painting.

1840–42 Study of art in Munich.

1845   Publication of his first poems under the title *Lieder eines Autodidakten.*

1848–50 Study at Heidelberg on a scholarship from the cantonal government of Zürich.

1850–55 Residence in Berlin.

1851   *Neuere Gedichte.*

1854–55 Publication of *Der grüne Heinrich* (a revised edition was published in 1880).

1856   First volume of *Die Leute von Seldwyla* (five stories, including *Romeo und Julia auf dem Dorfe*, *Die drei gerechten Kammacher* and *Spiegel, das Kätzchen*).

1861–76 Staatssekretär of the canton of Zürich.

1872   *Sieben Legenden.*

1874   Second volume of *Die Leute von Seldwyla* (including *Kleider machen Leute*).

1878   *Zürcher Novellen* (historical stories).

1883   *Gesammelte Gedichte.*

1890   Died in Zürich on 15th July.

A Village Romeo and Juliet

W ERE THIS TALE NOT BASED on actual occurrence, it would be mere idle repetition on my part to relate it. Yet how deeply rooted in human life is each and every one of the stories on which the great works of the past are built. For such stories, though few in number, constantly reappear in new guises and force themselves upon our attention.

From the banks of the beautiful river that flows past Seld- wyla, about half an hour's walk from the town, there rises a gentle ridge which, lush and fertile, merges into the rolling plain beyond. At the foot of the slope lies a village with a number of large farmsteads, and years ago three long fields used to stretch out side by side above it, like three giant ribbons.

One sunny September morning two farmers were away ploughing on the two outer fields; the field in the middle appeared to have lain fallow for many years, for it was full of stones and tall weeds, and a myriad creatures winged their untroubled way across its rustling grasses. The farmers, each tramping behind his plough, were tall, gaunt men of about forty who conveyed at first glance the air of prosperous and industrious husbandmen. They were wearing coarse knickerbockers whose every pleat had its permanent place, as though it were chiselled out of stone. Whenever they met some obstacle, they gripped the plough more tightly, and the sleeves of their rough shirts rippled under the strain; alert yet relaxed, their clean-shaven faces puckered slightly against the bright sunshine, they gauged their furrows, occasionally looking round when some distant sound disturbed the tranquillity of the scene.

Deliberately and with a certain natural grace they each moved forwards step by step. Neither of them spoke, save to give an order to the boy who was leading the fine horses. From a distance they looked identical representatives of the countryside at its most characteristic; to a closer view they appeared distinguishable only in that one had the flap of his white cap at the front, the other at the back. But this changed when they ploughed in the opposite direction, for as they met and passed at the top of the ridge, the strong east wind blew the cap of the one back over his head, while that of the other, who had the wind behind him, was blown forwards over his face. And at each turn there was a moment when the two caps stood erect quivering in the wind like two white tongues of flame.

Thus the two men worked peacefully on, affording a pleasant prospect in the stillness of the golden autumn landscape as they passed each other silently at the top of

the slope, drew further and further apart again and finally
vanished behind the ridge like two setting stars only to appear
again a short while later. If they found a stone in one of the
furrows, they tossed it on to the field in the middle, but this
happened only rarely, since almost all the stones that had ever
lain there were now piled up on this centre field.

The long morning had run part of its course when a neat little
cart was seen approaching the gentle slope from the village. It
was a tiny green perambulator in which the children of the
two farmers, a boy and a frail, delicate girl, were carrying up
the morning meal. For each man there was a tasty sandwich
wrapped in a serviette, a jug of wine and a glass, together
with a few extra trifles which the wives had sent along for
their hard-working husbands. Besides this, the perambulator
contained a motley assortment of odd-shaped apples and pears
which the children had found lying on the ground and started
to eat; and finally there was a one-legged doll with a dirty face
and no clothes, which was sitting between the sandwiches like
a lady of rank riding elegantly in her carriage.

After stopping many times on the way, the little conveyance
at last bumped its way to the top of the slope and stopped in
the shade of a linden bush at the edge of the field, where it
became possible to observe the two "coachmen" more closely.
The boy was seven, the girl five, both sound in wind and limb,
and the only striking feature about them was that they both

had very attractive eyes, while the girl's dark complexion and curly black hair gave her an intense, passionate look.

The farmers had now reached the top again. Stopping their ploughs in the half-completed furrow and leaving their horses some fodder, they walked across to where their meal was waiting and bade each other good morning, for they had not yet exchanged a word that day. As they sat there contentedly, good-humouredly sharing their food with the children, who did not leave, and after they had finished eating and drinking, they gazed out over the countryside and contemplated the smoke-shrouded village nestling in the hills: for when the people of Seldwyla cooked their tasty lunch, a silver haze hovered above the roofs of their houses, shining for miles around and floating serenely up into the mountains.

"Those rascals in Seldwyla are getting another good meal ready," said Manz, one of the farmers. Marti, the other, rejoined:

"Someone came to see me yesterday about this field."

"Someone from the Bezirksrat?"* asked Manz. "He came to my house too."

"Well, well. And I suppose he suggested that you should use the land and pay the council rent for it."

"Yes, until it is decided who owns it and what is to be done with it. But I refused to clear the place up for somebody else, and told them to sell the field and keep the money until the owner is found – which will probably never happen, because the authorities in Seldwyla take ages over everything, and in any case it is a difficult matter to settle. The rogues are all too eager to feather their own nests by renting the field. And it would be the same if they sold it – although you and I would take care not to drive the price too high! At least we would know then where we stood and who the land belonged to."

"That is just what I think, and I told the fellow so."

They were silent for a while, then Manz said:

"Still, it is a pity to see good ground left in this state. For almost twenty years nobody has troubled about it. There is no one in the village with any claim to it, nor does anyone know what has become of the children of that wastrel, the Trumpeter."

"Hm, a fine thing that would be!" retorted Marti. "Whenever I look at the Black Fiddler, who spends half this time with the gypsies and the other half playing for village dances, I could almost swear that he is one of the Trumpeter's grandchildren. Of course, he does not know that he owns the field, but what would he do with it? Get drunk on the proceeds for a month and then go on living as before! In any case, since no one can be sure, who is going to raise the subject?"

"And it might have unpleasant consequences," rejoined Manz. "We've already got enough on hand to prevent this wretched Fiddler from settling in our community. People are constantly trying to foist him on to us. If his parents went off to join the gypsies, let him stay there and scrape his fiddle for them. How in Heaven's name are we expected to know that he is the Trumpeter's grandson? Even if his swarthy face does remind me of the Trumpeter, I tell myself that no man is infallible, and the smallest scrap of paper, a mere fragment of a birth certificate, would satisfy my conscience better than a dozen wicked faces!"

"Quite right!" exclaimed Marti. "He says it is not his fault that he was not baptized, but does he expect us to carry our font out into the woods? We shall never do such a thing! Our font belongs in our church. If anything is to be carried around, let it be the bier that hangs outside on the church wall. The village is overcrowded already, and soon we shall need two more schoolteachers."

With this the farmers finished their meal and their conversation, and got up to resume their morning's work. The two children, who were going to return home with their fathers, pushed the cart into the shade of the little linden trees and embarked on an expedition into the strange wasteland with its creepers, its bushes and its piles of stones. After wandering hand in hand across the green wilderness for a while, joyfully swinging their arms over the tall thistle bushes, they sat down in the shade of one of these bushes, and the girl began to dress her doll with long leaves from the plants growing at the side of the path: she gave it a pretty green dress with jagged edges, and a bonnet made from a long red poppy that was still in bloom, tied on with a blade of grass. The little creature looked like a sorceress, and even more so when it was given a necklace and girdle of little red berries.

Setting it on top of the bush, they both regarded it for a while. Then the boy, tired of looking at it, knocked it down with a stone and disarranged its clothes. The girl quickly took them off in order to dress it again, but as the doll lay there, naked except for the red bonnet, the impetuous boy snatched it away from her and hurled it high into the air. With tears in her eyes she tried to catch it, but he caught it first, threw it up again and teased her as she vainly tried to get her hands on it.

As a result of this treatment, however, the doll's only leg became damaged at the knee, where grains of bran began to trickle through a little hole. As soon as the tormentor noticed the hole, he stopped, looked at it open-mouthed and eagerly began to widen it with his nails, so as to see where the bran came from. The girl became suspicious at his silence, rushed over to him and saw with horror what he was doing.

"Look!" he cried, swinging the doll round in front of her, so that the bran flew out into her face. With a scream she tried to reach it, imploring him to give it to her, but he ran away, swinging the miserable toy round and round until its leg hung down limply like an empty bag. Finally he flung it to the ground, putting on an air of haughty disdain as she threw herself tearfully on top of it and wrapped it in her apron. As she uncovered it again and saw its leg hanging down from its body like a salamander's tail, she started to cry afresh.

But seeing her weep so bitterly, the mischievous boy began to feel sorry for what he had done. When she saw him standing there repentant and uneasy, she suddenly stopped and hit him several times with the doll, whereupon he cried out "Ouch! Ouch!" and pretended to be hurt. So realistically did he do this, that she was appeased, and proceeded to help him dismember and destroy the doll. They bored hole after hole in it, letting the bran run out and carefully putting it in a heap on a flat stone, sifting it and looking at it closely.

The only part of the doll still intact was its head, which now claimed the children's particular attention. Removing it from its battered body, they peeped curiously into its interior. As they looked at the hollow cavity and at the bran, they were both seized by the same obvious thought, and raced each other to pour the bran into the head, which thereby came to have something in it for the first time. But the boy still seemed to regard this as useless knowledge, for suddenly he caught a large bluebottle, and while it buzzed inside his cupped hand, he told the girl to empty the bran out of the doll's head. Then he put the bluebottle inside and stuffed the head with grass. They held it to their ears and then stood it solemnly on a stone, where, still bedecked with the red poppy, and with the buzzing sound coming from it, it looked like an oracle, to whose parables and pronouncements the children listened in complete silence as they sat there together.

But every prophet evokes ingratitude and fear. The modicum of life in the pitiful little image aroused the children's cruel instincts, and they resolved to bury it alive. So they dug a hole and, without asking the insect's opinion, put the head in it and solemnly erected a cairn of stones at the head of the grave. But then they began to shudder at the thought that they had buried a real living creature, and they moved some distance away from the eerie spot. The little girl was tired and lay down on a soft, fragrant bank, chanting a few words in monotonous sequence, while the boy crouched beside her, wondering whether he too should lie down, so lazy and dreamy did he feel.

The sun shone down on her beautiful white teeth and crimson lips as she lay there singing. Holding her head in his hands and looking intently at her teeth, he said:

"Guess how many teeth you have!"

Pretending to count them up in her mind, she cried out impulsively:

"A hundred!"

"No, thirty-two!" he replied. "I'll count them!"

And he began to do so, but because he could never make them add up to thirty-two he kept starting over again. She lay still for a long time, then, since he could never finish his excited counting, she sat up and said:

"Now it's my turn to count yours!"

So he lay down on the grass with his mouth open, and she grasped his head and counted:

"One, two, seven, five, two, one…" for she had not yet learnt to count. The boy corrected her and taught her to count properly, so that time after time she too had to start again from the beginning. Of all the games they had played that day, this seemed to give them the greatest delight. Tired out at last, however, the little girl sank down on to the body of her mentor, and the two children fell asleep in the bright midday sunshine.

Meanwhile their fathers had finished ploughing, leaving behind them the fresh brown fields. As one of the boys came to the end of the last furrow and was about to stop, the farmer shouted:

"What are you stopping for? Turn round again!"

"But we've finished," protested the lad.

"Hold your tongue and do as you're told!" shouted the farmer.

So they turned round and carved a deep furrow in the middle field, sending the weeds and the stones flying up on both sides. The farmer did not stop to clear them away, apparently thinking there was plenty of time to do that later, but contented himself for the moment with getting the hardest part of the job done. So he ploughed up the gentle slope, and when he reached the top, where the breeze blew the tip of his cap backwards again, his neighbour passed him on the other side with his cap pointing forwards, also ploughing a wide furrow from the field in the middle and throwing up great clods of earth. Each saw clearly through what the other was doing but pretended not to. Passing each other without a word, they went their separate ways like two constellations setting beneath the horizon.

Thus do the shuttles of destiny pass back and forth, and as the saying goes, "What he weaves, no weaver knows".*

Harvest followed harvest, the children grew taller and more handsome each year, and the unclaimed field grew narrower and narrower under the two neighbours' ploughs. Neither man uttered a word about it, neither man even seemed to see what wrong he was doing. Along the whole length of the field the stones were piled up on an ever-dwindling strip in the middle, like a mountain ridge, and the wild creepers that grew on it were soon so high that, although the children had grown so tall, they could not see each other from their own sides.

They no longer went out to the field together, for Sali, as the ten-year-old Salomon was called, now took his place at the side of the youths and men, while the vivacious, dark-skinned Vrenchen was made to stay in the company of her own sex lest she should be laughed at for being a tomboy. Nevertheless, when everybody else was busy on the field, they clambered up on to the stony ridge that separated them and played at pushing each other down. Their fathers' fields met at no other point and since this was now the only contact that they had with each other, they seemed to celebrate the annual occasion all the more eagerly.

It had now been finally decided, however, that the field was to be sold and the money held in trust for the time being. The auction was held at the side of the field itself, but apart from Manz and Marti only a handful of idle bystanders were present, since nobody was interested in acquiring or cultivating this strange plot which separated the two neighbours. For although Manz and Marti were among the best farmers in the village, and had only acted as three-quarters of the rest would have done in the circumstances, people looked at them uneasily and had no desire to own the narrow strip which lay between their two fields. Most men are willing to commit certain common misdeeds if the temptation is put under their noses. But when one man has committed such a misdeed, the others are relieved that it was he who did it and not they, and that the temptation had not been theirs. They make the offender into a yardstick by which to measure their own sins, and treat him with modest deference as the one singled out by the gods to bear the common guilt; yet at the same time their mouths water at the thought of the pleasures that he has enjoyed.

Thus Manz and Marti were the only ones who bid seriously for the field. After a considerable struggle Manz finally succeeded in outbidding his neighbour, and the field was knocked down to him. The officials and the onlookers left the scene, and the two farmers, who both intended to finish some work on their fields, met as they moved away.

"I suppose," said Marti, "you will now put your fields together, the old one and the new, and divide them into two equal parts. At least, that is what I would do if I had bought the thing."

"That's just what I'm going to do," replied Marti. "As a single field it would be too big. But there's something I wanted to say to you. I noticed the other day that at the bottom of this field that now belongs to me, you had driven your plough in from the side and cut off quite a fair-sided triangular piece. You probably thought that the whole field would soon become yours in any case. But as it now belongs to me, you will realize that I cannot have a crooked edge like that in it, so you can hardly object if I straighten it again. We shan't quarrel over that."

"I see no cause for quarrel either," replied Marti in the same even tone. "As far as I am concerned, you have bought the field as it stands now. We all inspected it an hour ago, and since then it hasn't changed in the slightest."

"Fiddlesticks!" cried Manz. "What's past is past! But sometimes matters go too far, and when all is said and done, a thing has to be properly settled. Right from the beginning these two fields have been dead straight. What strange quirk is it that makes you want to introduce such an ugly shape? What sort of reputation would we get if we left it crooked? The odd corner has simply got to go!"

Marti laughed and retorted:

"What a remarkable concern you suddenly show that people might laugh at you! Still, I suppose you can do it if you want to, though the crooked line does not worry me in the least. So if it annoys you, let's make it straight, but not on my side – and I'll put that in writing if you want it!"

"There's no point in joking," said Manz. "It is going to be made straight, and on your side, too. So you can put that in your pipe and smoke it!"

"We'll see about that," snapped Marti, and the two men parted company without another glance, each glaring in front of him as though his whole attention were riveted on something in the distance.

The next day Manz sent out a farmhand, a servant girl and his own son Sali to the field to pull up the weeds and the briers and put them on to heaps so that it would be easier to carry the stones away later. That Sali, who was barely eleven years old and had never been made to do any manual work before, should now be sent out with the others in spite of his mother's protestations, signified a change in his father's nature. He accompanied this decision with soft and soothing words, as though wishing to use his harshness towards his own flesh and blood as a means of quelling the sense of injustice which ruled his life and now began to run its slow, sinister course.

Cheerfully the little group pulled up the weeds and hacked away busily at the mass of strange plants and bushes which had grown up there over the years. It was the sort of unorganized work that required no particular care or skill but was looked on rather as enjoyment. All this foliage, dried out by the sun, was piled up and burned with great jubilation; the smoke was blown far and wide, and the young folk leapt about like souls possessed.

This was the last celebration that the ill-starred field was to know. Young Vrenchen, Marti's daughter, also came out

GOTTFRIED KELLER

to help with the work. The unusualness of the occasion and the air of excitement that surrounded it were good enough reasons for her to join her young playmate again, and the two children were cheerful and happy as they danced round the fire. Other children came as well, making a joyful party. But whenever Sali became separated from Vrenchen, he tried to hunt her out again, while she too, laughing with delight, always managed to slip back to him, so that they both felt that this wonderful day should never be allowed to end.

Towards evening old Manz arrived to see how the work had progressed, and although they had already finished, he scolded them for their frivolity and broke up the celebrations.

At the same time Marti appeared on his field. Catching sight of his daughter, he put his fingers in his mouth and let out a shrill, imperious whistle. She hastened across to his side, and without really knowing why, he gave her a few sound cuffs on the head. The two children burst into tears and made their way sadly home, knowing as little why they were now so miserable as why they had been so happy a moment ago. In their innocence they could not understand the reason for this streak of cruelty that had recently appeared in their fathers' characters, and it therefore did not arouse any deeper emotions in them.

For the harder work of the next few days, when Manz had the stones shovelled up and carted away, the farmhands were

18

needed. It was an endless task: all the stones in the world seemed to have collected there. But instead of removing them from the field altogether, he had each cartload emptied on to the disputed triangular area which Marti had carefully ploughed. Drawing a straight line to mark the boundary, he dumped on to this little piece of land all the stones which they had both thrown over for as long as they could remember. The result was a large pyramid which he was convinced his adversary would do nothing to remove.

This was the last thing that Marti had bargained for; in fact, he had reckoned that the other man would go on ploughing as usual. He had therefore waited at home until he saw Manz go out, and only when the job was almost done did he hear about the fine monument that Marti had erected. Livid with rage, he rushed out, saw the hideous pile of stones, rushed back again and fetched the bailiff in order to register an immediate protest and have the land officially requisitioned. From this moment onwards the two men were locked in continuous legal battle, and did not rest until they had brought about their utter ruin and destruction.

Wise and reasonable as they normally were, Manz and Marti were now incapable of seeing beyond their own noses. The most petty legalistic thoughts filled their minds, and neither had the ability or the desire to understand how the other could behave in such a palpably unjust manner and wilfully appropriate this miserable bit of land to himself. In addition, Manz had a remarkable sense of symmetry, and was deeply offended by the stupid obstinacy with which Marti insisted on preserving the senseless and arbitrary crookedness of the field.

They each shared the conviction, however, that the other, in his impertinent and insolent way, must consider him a despicable fool, since one could only mete out such treatment to an unprincipled rogue, never to an upright citizen. Each thus felt his honour peculiarly offended and gave himself up passionately to the quarrel and to the resulting moral corruption. Their lives became like the tortured dream of two condemned souls who fight with each other on a narrow plank which is drifting down a murky stream: they beat the air, then, in the belief that they have laid hands on their own misery, seize and finally destroy each other.

Since their entire case was corrupt, they both fell a ready prey to the worst kinds of trickster, who inflamed their perverted imaginations and filled their minds with the most despicable thoughts. Most of these enterprising gentry, for whom the whole affair was a gift from the gods, belonged to the town of Seldwyla, and in a short time the two enemies each had their retinue of mediators, scandal-mongers and advisers who knew a hundred ways of relieving a man of his money.

The little triangle of land with its pile of stones, on the top of which a forest of thistles and nettles had already started to grow, had now become merely the seed, the starting point, of a disordered situation and a meaningless life, in which these two fifty-year-old men adopted attitudes and habits, hopes and principles, quite different from those by which they had lived hitherto. The more money they wasted, the more eagerly they sought after it; and the less each had, the more determined he grew to outdo his neighbour in getting rich. They were taken in by every fraud, and year in, year out, they bet on all the lotteries in the country, whose tickets circulated in Seldwyla in large numbers.

But they never won a penny. Instead, they kept hearing of other people's success and of how they themselves had almost won. Yet this passion continued to provide a regular outlet for their money, and sometimes the inhabitants of Seldwyla played a trick on them by having them share the same lottery ticket, so that they both set their hopes for ruining each other on one and the same number.

Half their time they spent in the town of Seldwyla, each establishing himself in some dingy cafe. Allowing their tempers to become inflamed, they were persuaded to part with their money in the most shameful ways and to give themselves over to a dissipated life of carousing. Yet at the same time they were sick at heart, for whereas they were really only carrying on the quarrel so as not to be taken for fools, they were now regarded by everyone as two of the biggest fools that had ever lived.

For the other half of the time they either stayed sullenly at home or went about their work, trying feverishly to make up for the time they had wasted and driving away all their good and trustworthy labourers in the process.

Things went rapidly from bad to worse. They were soon heavily in debt and clinging desperately to what was left to them, as vulnerable and as insecure as one-legged storks at the mercy of the wind. But however bad things became, the hatred between them grew ever greater for each regarded the other as the sole cause of his misfortune, his arch-enemy, the adversary whom the Devil had deliberately sent into the world to wreak his downfall. Even if they caught sight of each other from a distance, they would spit on the ground, and all contact between wives, children and servants was forbidden on pain of the severest punishment.

The two women reacted in different ways to the situation. Marti's wife, a good, upright woman, could not endure it, and died of grief before her daughter had reached the age of fourteen.

Manz's wife, on the other hand, adapted herself to the change, and needed only to give free rein to certain inborn feminine frailties for them to turn into vices, and encourage her to share in her husband's evil ways. Her penchant for dainty sweetmeats became gluttony, and she turned her volubility to false flattery and slander, saying the opposite of what she really thought, setting people against each other and deceiving her husband wherever she could. The frankness with which she used to indulge in innocent gossip now became brazen arrogance, and instead of submitting to her husband, she began to make him look a fool; if he resisted, she became even more aggressive, and lost no opportunity to present herself as the true master of her degenerate household.

Such was the tragic situation in which the two children grew up, with neither happiness in their youth nor joyful hope for the future, since they were surrounded by nothing but strife and sorrow. Vrenchen's position was probably the unhappier, for her mother was dead, and, alone in the desolate house, she was at the mercy of her barbaric and tyrannical father.

She was now sixteen, a slim, delicate girl, the curls of her chestnut hair almost reaching down to her shining brown eyes, and the crimson of her cheeks and lips glowing beneath her swarthy skin to give her an appearance unusual for a dark-skinned child. Every fibre in her body quivered with life, and she was ready for sport and play whenever the weight of her care and suffering would lift from her mind.

But moods of depression came upon her only too often. Not only had she to bear the grief and ever-growing misery of the family but also had to care for herself and keep herself decently dressed, although her father was reluctant to give her any money to do so. It was only with the greatest difficulty that she was able to come by a cheap Sunday dress for her slim form, or a few worthless coloured neckerchiefs. In every way she was made to feel humble and underprivileged, and at no time could she have fallen a victim to pride. In addition, she had been old enough to know how her mother had suffered, and this put a further check on her natural exuberance. Thus whenever, in spite of this, she was seen to welcome the slightest ray of sunshine that fell across her path, she presented a touching picture of innocence and charm.

At first sight Sali did not appear to be so deeply affected. He was a strong, handsome youth who could not be suspected, at least from his physical appearance, of having been ill-treated. He must have seen how disgracefully his parents were behaving, and he seemed to recall a time when things were different; indeed, he still had a clear memory of his father as an honest, wise and peaceful farmer, the same man that he now saw as a stupid greybeard, an idler and a quarreller, who raged and boasted and frittered his life away in base and foolish ventures, sliding further down the path of ruin with every step.

This angered Sali, however, and he often felt a sense of grief and shame that it should be so, although in the inexperience of youth he could not understand how things had come to this pass. Yet his worries were softened by the flattering manner in which his mother treated him, for in order to have somebody who would stand by her in her pursuit of her evil ways, and also to satisfy her urge to boast and swagger, she let him have whatever he wished, bought him showy new clothes and encouraged him to enjoy himself in whatever way he liked.

He accepted the situation with no great feeling of gratitude, for he knew that his mother was a liar and a gossip. He indulged his fancy with complete freedom but took no great pleasure in doing so. Still feeling a youth's desire for a settled and reasonably useful life, he was as yet untainted by the evil example of his parents. Indeed, he was almost exactly as his father had been at that age, and as a result the latter felt a spontaneous respect for his son, in whom, through his perplexity of conscience, he relived the tortured yet cherished memory of his own childhood.

But in spite of the freedom that he enjoyed, Sali was not really happy, realizing that he had no training for the future – for any rational pattern of work in Manz's house had long since been abandoned. He thus found his chief consolation in the thought of his independence and hitherto blameless conduct. Priding himself on this, he watched sullenly as the days went by, averting his gaze from what lay in the future.

The sole obligation in his life was to continue his father's hostility towards Marti and everything connected with him. All he knew was that Marti had offended his father and that the same enmity persisted in Marti's house, so it was not difficult for him both to ignore Marti and his daughter, and to play the role of a young, if somewhat gentle antagonist himself.

Vrenchen, however, who had more to suffer than Sali and led a far lonelier life, felt less drawn to an attitude of rigid hostility and believed only that the well-dressed and seemingly happier Sali scorned her. She thus tried to keep out of his sight, and whenever he was close at hand, she hurried away, and he did not even bother to look in her direction. So a number of years went by without his seeing her at close quarters, and he no longer had any real idea what she looked like. Yet he often felt very curious to know, and whenever the Martis were mentioned, he involuntarily thought of the daughter whom he would now no longer recognize but whose memory was far from displeasing.

However, it was his father Manz who was the first of the two enemies to break. He was forced to leave his house; his wife had helped him squander his money, and his son had also had certain needs to fulfil, whilst Marti was the only consumer in his own tottering empire – for although his daughter was allowed to work like a slave, she was not allowed to have any wants. So, following the advice of his supporters in Seldwyla, Manz moved into the town and set himself up as an innkeeper.

It is always sad to see a farmer, accustomed to country life, move into the town with what he has salvaged of his possessions, and open a café or a bar, desperately trying to play the busy, genial publican while his personal feelings are anything but genial.

Only when Manz and his family moved out of their farmhouse did it become evident how poor they had become, for the dilapidated furniture which they loaded up betrayed that they had not bought or repaired anything for years. Nevertheless, his wife put on her best clothes and took her place on top of the lumber cart, already seeing herself as a town lady and looking down scornfully at her fellow villagers who peeped out from behind the hedges as the pitiful procession went by. She had made up her mind that she would captivate the whole town with her wit and charm, and that what her simpleton of a husband could not do, she would accomplish herself once she was established in a fine hostelry as the mistress of the establishment.

In fact, the hostelry turned out to be a miserable tavern in a remote and dingy little alley: the previous occupant had gone bankrupt, and the authorities were leasing it to Manz in the hope that they would thereby recoup the few hundred talers that were still outstanding. They also sold him a few casks of diluted wine and the equipment belonging to the inn – a dozen cheap bottles and glasses, and a few deal tables and benches which had once been painted red but were now badly battered and scratched. An iron ring, in which there was a carving of a hand pouring red wine from a jug into a glass, grated to and fro on a hook in front of the window, and above the front door hung a shrivelled sprig of holly.

Manz did not share his wife's complacency, and as though sensing his impending doom, he savagely whipped up the half-starved horses which he had borrowed from the new owner of his farm. His last wretched servant boy had deserted him weeks before.

As he drove off, he saw the gloating, mocking figure of Marti pretending to busy himself with something at the roadside, and he cursed him as the sole cause of his misfortune. Sali, meanwhile, as soon as the can was on its way, quickened his steps and went ahead, making his own way to the town through side-lanes.

"Here we are!" cried Manz, as the cart drew up in front of the dingy tavern. His wife was taken aback, for the place was a truly sorry sight. People hastened to their doors and windows to see the new farmer-turned-landlord, putting on expressions of scorn and pity in their haughty manner.

Climbing down from the cart, Manz's wife ran into the house, her eyes filling with angry tears. She had no wish to show herself again that day, for she was ashamed of the battered furniture and shabby beds which were now being unloaded. Sali was ashamed too, but was made to help his father unload their possessions in the alley, where ragged children began to climb about on the strange-looking pile and poke fun at the farmer and his downtrodden family.

The inside of the house was even more depressing, and looked for all the world like a robbers' den. The damp, dirty walls had been hastily painted with cheap lime, and apart from the dark and dingy bar-saloon with its peeling red tables, the house consisted of nothing but a few miserable little bedrooms in which, as everywhere, the previous occupants had left behind the filthiest mess imaginable.

Such was the way Manz's new life started, and such was the way it went on. During the first few weeks, particularly in the evenings, a group of neighbours might arrive who were curious to see the new landlord and whether there was any entertainment to be had there.

The landlord did not claim their attention for long: crude, graceless, boorish and unfriendly, Manz was not capable of decent behaviour, nor did he desire to be. Slowly and clumsily he filled the glasses and placed them sullenly in front of his customers, muttering a few inaudible words.

To make up for this, his wife threw herself into her task with all the more zest, and actually managed to attract a few customers for a while, though for reasons that she little guessed. She was a portly matron, and had put together a costume which she was convinced made her irresistible. This consisted of an unbleached linen skirt, a green silk spencer, a cotton apron and an untidy white ruff. She had rolled her thin hair into ridiculous little curls above her forehead and planted a large comb in the plait at the back. With a forced air of grace she waddled and floundered about, pouting stupidly in what she thought was a charming manner, tripped up to the tables with mincing gait and put down the glass or the plate of cheese, exclaiming with a smile: "All right? Everything all right? Very good, sir! Very good, sir!" and making other stupid comments. Normally she was not at a loss for words, but now, since she was a stranger to the town, she was incapable of saying anything intelligent.

The rough townsfolk sitting there nudged each other under the table and almost exploded with laughter, holding their heads in their hands and spluttering:

"My goodness, what a creature!"

"An absolute jewel!" cried another. "It was well worth coming here! We've not seen anything like this for ages!"

Manz observed them, glowering. Then he dug his wife in the ribs and whispered:

"You stupid fool! What do you think you're up to?"

"Leave me alone, you clumsy idiot!" she cried indignantly. "Can't you see that I know how to get on with people? In any case, these are only rabble that you have brought in. I'll soon have better class customers in here, you'll see!"

The only light there was in the room came from a few thin tallow candles. Sali, who had heard this exchange, went out into the dark kitchen and sat down by the stove, weeping bitterly.

The guests soon tired of the spectacle of Frau Manz, and went back to places where they felt more at ease and could have a good laugh about it. Now and again a stranger might come in for a drink and stare vacantly at the bare walls around him; sometimes even a group of people arrived, raising false hopes with their jollity and excitement.

After a while the couple began to grow frightened in their gloomy house. The sun hardly ever penetrated into its rooms, and Manz, who had formerly spent half his time in the town, now began to find this confinement unbearable. When the thought of the wide, open fields came to him, he scowled morosely at the ceiling or the floor, sprang up and went to the tiny front door, only to rush back again when he saw the neighbours peering at "the surly landlord", as they called him.

Soon they were in a state of abject poverty. In order to get anything to eat, they had to wait till someone came and paid a few coppers for a glass or two of such wine as was left; and if he asked for a sausage or something else to eat, it often cost them a great deal of trouble to obtain it. The only wine they had left was in a single large bottle which they secretly filled at another inn. They were tavern-keepers without bread or wine, trying to wear cheerful faces while having empty stomachs. Indeed, they were almost thankful when nobody came and they could sit huddled together in the deserted saloon and drag out their pitiful existence in a no-man's-land between life and death.

When Manz's wife finally realized the bitter truth, she took off her green spencer, and, as she had formerly been governed by her faults, so now, in the hour of trial, she began to reveal her virtues. Patiently she tried to keep up her husband's morale and instruct her son in the ways of good living, making many sacrifices and trying in her own way to exert a beneficent influence which, however limited, was at least better than nothing, or than an influence of the opposite kind, and helped to prevent things breaking up altogether. She offered advice, to the best of her ability, on all manner of problems, and even if her advice was useless or mistaken, she bore the men's anger patiently. In short, she practised in her old age all the virtues she should have cultivated in her youth.

In order to get some food, and also to while away the time, Manz and his son took to fishing in the river at places where it was permitted. This was a favourite pastime of penniless Seldwylans. When weather conditions were favourable and the fish could be expected to bite, dozens of men set out with rod and bucket, and an angler would be found every few steps along the river bank. One would be standing barefoot in the water, wearing a long brown overcoat, another, in a tight-fitting blue tailcoat and with an old felt hat pulled down over one ear, would take up position in an old willow tree. Further along there was even a man fishing in a torn floral dressing gown – the only outer garment he possessed – with a long pipe in one hand and his fishing rod in the other. And round the next bend a fat, bald-headed old man was standing stark naked on a stone and fishing; but although standing in the water, he had such dirty feet that it looked as if he still had his boots on.

Each man had a little jar or can full of wriggling worms which he had dug up on some previous occasion. At dusk, when the weather was sultry and the sky had clouded over, indicating the approach of rain, these characters stood in their profusion at the side of the running stream, as motionless as a row of statues of saints or prophets. The farmers drove past without heeding them, so did the boatman on the river, whose craft disturbed the water and made the anglers swear under their breath.

Twelve years earlier, when he was ploughing on the slope above the river behind his fine team of horses, Manz would have been furious if anyone had suggested that he would eventually take his place among this motley crew. He hurried round behind them and moved upstream, like some capricious shadow from the underworld seeking a cosy nook for itself by the dark waters of the infernal shades. But neither he nor his son had the patience to stand with a rod in his hand, and they recalled how the farmers used to catch fish with their hands. So, taking their rods with them as a pretence, they walked along the banks of the stream where they knew there were valuable trout to be had.

Marti's affairs, in the meantime, had also gone from bad to worse. He was bored with life, and instead of working on his neglected land, he, too, had been lured into fishing, and spent days on end splashing about in the water. Vrenchen was not allowed to leave his side, but, whatever the weather, had to carry his tackle for him through pools, streams and boggy fields, leaving all the important tasks at home undone. There was now no one left but the two of them: for since Marti only had a few acres left which he and his daughter cultivated either indifferently or not at all, he needed no help.

One evening, when storm clouds were gathering overhead, he was walking along a deep, fast-flowing stream in which the trout were leaping high. Suddenly he saw his enemy Manz coming towards him on the other bank, and was filled with scorn and rage at the sight of him. They had not approached so close to each other for years, except in courts of law, where they had to restrain their insults, and Marti shouted out in fury:

"What are you doing here, you cur? Why don't you stay in your miserable hovel?"

"Just you wait, you blackguard!" cried Manz. "If you're down to catching fish, it will soon be all up with you!"

The rushing of the stream grew louder, and Marti had to shout to make himself heard.

"Shut your mouth, you scoundrel!" he shrieked. "It was you that ruined me!"

As the storm wind rose, the willows at the water's edge began to sway violently to and fro, and Manz could hardly be heard above the noise.

"I'd be only too glad if I had, you miserable wretch!" he shouted.

"You dog!" cried Marti.

"You stupid idiot!" Manz bellowed back.

Marti rushed along the bank like a wild animal and looked for a place to cross. He was the more furious of the two because he believed that, as an innkeeper, Manz must at least have had enough to eat and drink and be leading a reasonably comfortable life, whilst he, Marti, was unjustly condemned to the monotony of his broken-down farmstead.

In a fine rage himself, Manz stalked along on the opposite bank. Behind him walked Sali who, instead of listening to the angry quarrel, looked across in curiosity and surprise at Vrenchen, who was following her father and staring in shame at the ground in front of her so that her curly brown hair fell down over her face. In one hand she carried a wooden fish bucket, while with the other she had been carrying her shoes and stockings, and holding up her skirt to keep it from getting wet. On Sali's approach she lowered it in embarrassment; yet if she had looked up, she would have seen that Sali no longer looked proud and superior, but was himself utterly downcast.

While Vrenchen fixed her eyes dejectedly on the ground, and Sali could do nothing but stare at the slim, graceful figure, neither of them noticed that the two men, who had now stopped shouting at each other, were running furiously towards a wooden bridge which had just come into view. The storm was breaking, and flashes lit up the eerie, dismal scene. The thunder began to roll through the dark grey clouds, and heavy drops of rain were falling as the men rushed on to the little bridge. As it swayed to and fro under their weight, they grabbed each other savagely and began to strike each other with their fists, their faces livid and distorted with rage.

It is not a pleasant sight to see sober-minded men brought to a point where, whether from aggressiveness, rashness or mere self-defence, they become involved in a fight against people with whom they have no real quarrel. But this is nothing in comparison with the pitiful prospect of two mature men who have known each other for years being driven by a personal hatred to lay hands on each other.

Yet such was the state to which these two ageing men had degenerated. The last time they had fought was fifty years ago; since then neither had touched the other save to shake hands as friends, and this only rarely, since they were phlegmatic and independent by nature.

After aiming a few blows at each other, they began to wrestle, snarling and groaning as they tried to throw each other over the creaking handrail into the water below. The children had now caught up with them, and Sali jumped ahead to help his father put an end to his hated enemy, who appeared to be the weaker of the two and on the verge of collapse. Vrenchen dropped everything she was carrying and rushed screaming to her father's side, holding him in her arms to protect him, but only hampering him in his struggle. The tears streamed from her eyes and she looked imploringly at Sali, who was on the point of seizing Marti and finally overpowering him.

Then, as though by instinct, he gripped his own father, trying to quieten him and get him away from his enemy. This brought a brief pause in the struggle, while all four swayed to and fro on the bridge.

As they fought to separate their parents, the two children came close to each other. At that moment a ray of sunlight glinted through a gap in the clouds, and Sali saw before him the face that he had known so well but which had since taken on a fresh beauty. Vrenchen saw his astonishment, and gave him a fleeting smile through her tears. Pitting his strength against that of his father, Sali finally succeeded in getting him away from Marti and persuading him to desist. When the two men regained their breath, they turned away from each other and began again to curse and swear. The anxious children kept silent, but as the two groups parted, they quickly clasped each other's hands, cold and wet from the water and the fish, without their parents noticing.

The clouds had now closed in again; it was getting darker and darker, and the rain came down in torrents as the angry farmers went their way. Manz, shivering in the cold, trudged homeward through the dark, wet lanes, his hands in his pockets, bowing his head before the driving rain, and tears, which he had dared not wipe away lest his son should notice them, trickled down his cheeks.

But Sali saw nothing. Blissfully happy, he noticed neither wind nor rain, neither darkness nor grief, and felt as rich and carefree as a prince. He was haunted by the vision of the brief smile on Vrenchen's face, and only now, over half an hour later, did he return it, giving a tender smile to the rain and the darkness, and cherishing the thought that she could not but feel his presence and step out of the shadows to greet him.

The following day Manz was so shaken that he would not leave the house. His feud, added to the misery of recent years, took on a harsher aspect and pervaded the whole oppressive atmosphere of the shabby house. Manz and his wife wandered listlessly and despondently from the bar into the gloomy rooms behind, from there into the kitchen, and from the kitchen back into the bar, to which no customer ever came. In the end they would each sit in a corner and pick some meaningless quarrel, falling asleep from time to time, and waking to the thoughts of an uneasy conscience.

But Sali saw nothing of this, for his thoughts were only of Vrenchen. Since the events of the previous day he had not only felt unbelievably rich but also seemed to have experienced a sensation of indescribable beauty and goodness. This experience had been visited upon him from above and was the source of an unceasing wonderment and happiness, yet he seemed to have been aware of it all along. Nothing can be compared with the bliss that comes to one in human shape – a personal shape with its own God-given name.

This day Sali felt neither idle nor unhappy, neither poor nor abandoned. For hour after hour he toiled to conjure up in his mind the vision of Vrenchen's face, but so feverish were his attempts that he almost lost sight of her and began to believe that the vision would never return. Yet she seemed to be for ever before his eyes: he felt the warmth of her presence, and seemed to be in the power of something that he had only seen once and did not understand. In his happiness he could clearly recall her features as a little girl but not those which he had seen the day before. Had he never seen her again, his imagination would have had to put her picture together piece by piece until it was complete. But now that his eyes had claimed their own joyful role in this task, his wily imagination obstinately refused to play its part. So as the afternoon sun streamed into the upper storeys of the dark houses, he stepped out through the door and wandered off towards his old home, which he now saw as a heavenly Jerusalem with twelve shining gates, and the closer he came to it, the faster his heart beat.

On his way he passed Vrenchen's father walking towards Seldwyla. Wild and untidy, his beard grey and unkempt, he wore the vindictive mien of one who had frittered away his own possessions and was now intent on bringing ruin upon others. Yet as he passed him, Sali felt not hatred but fear and apprehension, as though his fate rested in the hands of this old farmer, from whom he would rather have received his life as a gift than wrenched it from him as a prize.

But Marti just gave him a vicious glance and went his way. This was as Sali wished, however, for as he watched the figure moving away from him, he began to realize the true nature of his own feelings. Slipping unobtrusively through paths on the outskirts of the village, which he had known from childhood, he soon found himself in front of Marti's farmhouse.

It was years since he had seen the place from close quarters, for even while they were still living here, the rival families avoided entering each other's land. Sali stared in amazement at the desolate scene. Marti had been forced to sell his fields one by one, and there was now nothing left but the house itself and the yard in front of it, together with an area of garden and the one field by the river, to which he was obstinately clinging as long as he could. But he made no attempt at proper cultivation, and on the field where the lines of golden corn used to wave at harvest time, all manner of odd seeds left over in bags and boxes had been planted – turnips, cabbage and the like, together with a few potatoes. The whole impression was of a carelessly tended vegetable patch from which he could eke out a hand-to-mouth existence – here a handful of turnips, there a clump of potatoes or cabbages, and the rest left to grow wild or to rot. People walked in or out of it at will, and what had formerly been a fine large field was now almost indistinguishable from the disputed strip of wasteland from which the whole tragedy stemmed.

The area round the house was no longer farmed. The stable was empty, the door swung to and fro on one hinge, and across the dark entrance thousands of half-grown spiders wove their glistening webs in the sunlight. By the open door of the barn, which used to house the rich harvest, hung some cheap fishing tackle, the tools of Marti's poaching. Not a hen or a pigeon, not a cat or a dog was to be seen in the yard; the only living thing left was the fountain, but instead of flowing through the pipe, the water was seeping out through a hole and collecting in puddles on the ground, symbolizing to perfection the spirit of decay.

It would not have cost Marti much effort to mend the hole in the pipe. But Vrenchen was made to struggle to get herself clean water from these foul conditions and wash her clothes in the puddles instead of in the washtub, which stood there cracked and dried up.

The house itself presented an equally lamentable appearance. Many of the windows were broken and patched up with strips of paper; yet the panes were probably the friendliest thing about the whole melancholy scene, for they were all polished and spotlessly clean, even the broken ones, and shone like Vrenchen's own eyes, which brought to the dark, dilapidated house the only brightness that it had. And like the curly hair that surrounded her eyes, and the orange cotton neckerchiefs she wore, so the wild creeper twined its way round the shining windows and along the walls, merging with a mass of swaying beanstalks and a fragrant cluster of orange wallflowers. The beans were clinging to rakes or brooms stuck upside down in the ground, and twined round the rusty pike which Vrenchen's grandfather had used when he was a sergeant in the cavalry. More beans were growing up a battered ladder which had stood for ages against the side of the house, and were hanging down in front of the brightly polished windows like the curls above Vrenchen's eyes.

The farmyard, now more picturesque than practical, stood somewhat apart from the neighbouring houses, and at this moment there was not a soul in sight, so without fear of being seen, Sali leant against an old shed some distance away and looked steadily across at the silent, ramshackle building.

After a while Vrenchen appeared at the door and stared out for a long time, as though meditating. Sali stood motionless, his eyes fixed on her. At last she turned her head and saw him. They stared at each other as though they had seen a mirage. Then Sali began to walk slowly across towards her. Stretching out her arms to him, she whispered:

"Sali."

Gazing into her eyes, he gripped her hands. As she reddened, tears sprang to her eyes.

"What do you want?" she said in low tones.

"Just to see you," he answered. "Let us be friends again!"

"And our parents?" she murmured, turning her tear-stained face away.

"Are we to blame for what they have done and what they have made of their lives?" he cried. "If we two stay together and care for each other, perhaps we can make up for all the misery they have caused."

"No good would ever come of it," replied Vrenchen with a sigh. "You must go your own way, Sali."

"Are you alone?" he asked. "May I not come in for a moment?"

"Father told me he was going into Seldwyla to teach your father a lesson. But you must not stay, because someone might see you when you leave. So please go now, while nobody is about."

"No, I will not!" cried Sali. "I have been thinking of you ever since yesterday, and I am not leaving until we have talked to each other at least for a little while. It will do us good!"

Vrenchen hesitated for a moment. Then she said:

"I shall have to go out to our field this evening to fetch some vegetables. You know the field I mean – it is the only one we still have. Nobody will be there, because the others are working somewhere else. Meet me there if you want to. But go away now, and be careful that no one sees you. People no longer have any dealings with us round here, but their gossip would soon reach my father's ears."

They let go of each other's hands, only to grasp them again and exclaim with one breath:

"But how are you?"

Instead of replying, they stammered out their question again, while the answer was to be seen in the look in their eyes. As is the way with lovers, the words would not come, and half blissful, half sorrowful, they hurriedly parted.

"I will come soon!" cried Vrenchen, as Sali went away.

So he went out to the quiet ridge where the two fields lay spread out peacefully. The bright July sunshine, the white clouds billowing above the acres of ripe, waving corn, the sparkling blue river wending its way through the valley – for the first time in years everything filled him with joy instead of sadness, and he threw himself full-length in the shade of the cornfield at the edge of Marti's desolate waste and looked up happily up at the sky.

Barely a quarter of an hour had passed, during which his thoughts had been only of his childhood sweetheart, when he saw her standing in front of him, smiling down on him as he lay there. He sprang up in joy.

"Vreeli!" he cried.

Still smiling she stretched out her arms towards him, and hand in hand they walked along the side of the swaying corn down towards the river, exchanging only an occasional word. Happily they strolled back and forth, like a constellation rising and setting behind the sunlit curve of the ridge over which the straight furrows of their father's ploughs had once run.

Suddenly, as they raised their eyes from the blue corn-flowers on the ground before them, they became aware of another, sinister body on the horizon of their world, a dark figure who had appeared from nowhere. Vrenchen trembled at the thought that he might have been lying in the corn, and Sali whispered, aghast:

"The Black Fiddler!"

The man striding along in front of them carried a fiddle and a bow under his arm, and presented a wild, swarthy appearance. He was wearing a small black felt hat and a dirty black smock, and his hair and the stubble on his chin were also jet-black. His face and hands, too, looked black, for he performed all manner of menial jobs: he was a tinker by trade but also helped the charcoal-burners and tar-workers in the woods, and only took to his fiddle when there was an easy penny to be earned among the farmers who were making merry in some tavern or holding a celebration.

Sali and Vrenchen crept along behind him, hoping that he would leave the field without looking round. And it seemed that he would, for he behaved as though he had not noticed them. Some strange compulsion prevented them from venturing away from the narrow path and forced them to follow the mysterious figure right to the end of the field, where the cruel pile of stones still stood on the disputed corner of land. A mass of corn poppies had taken root on it, making it look like a mountain on fire.

All of a sudden the Black Fiddler leapt with a single bound on to the top of the stones, turned and looked about him. The couple stopped in their tracks and looked up at him in confusion. They could not go on, because the path would have led them into the village, yet they did not want to turn back in full view of him.

Looking at them sharply, he cried:

"I know who you are! You are the children of the men who stole this field from me! I am delighted to see how prosperous you have become. I'll live to see the end of you yet, just you wait! Look at me, you poor little creatures! What do you think of my nose, eh?"

His nose was indeed a frightening sight, protruding sharply from his features like a bludgeon which had been thrown into his black, bony face. Beneath it was a small round hole for a mouth, from which came a perpetual puffing, hissing and whistling. Even his little hat contributed something to his uncanny appearance, for it was neither round nor pointed but seemed to change shape every few moments. Only the whites of his eyes could be seen as they flashed to and fro, like two rabbits darting hither and thither.

"Look at me!" he cried in an imperious tone. "Your fathers know me well, and all the villagers recognize me as soon as they see my nose. Years ago it was announced that there was a sum of money due to the heir of this field. Twenty times I claimed it, but I have neither birth certificate nor proof of citizenship, and no one will accept the testimony of the gypsies who were present at my birth. So the time limit expired, and I was swindled out of the money that rightfully belonged to me and with which I could have left here. I begged your fathers to confirm my claim, for their conscience must have told them that I was the true heir. But they chased me out of the house, and now they have gone to the Devil themselves! Well, that's the way of the world, and I am prepared to accept it. So if you want to dance, I'll play for you!"

Whereupon he jumped down on the other side of the stones and made off towards the village, where the harvest was being brought in and the people were in high spirits.

When he had gone, the young couple sat down dejectedly on the stones, let go of each other's hands and hung their heads in sorrow. The Fiddler's words had shaken them out of their childish trance, and as they sat there in their misery, the rose-like hue of their life clouded over, and their spirits became as heavy as the stones on which they sat.

Then Vrenchen suddenly remembered the Fiddler's strange face and nose, and could not help laughing.

"What a comical sight the poor man is! What a nose!" she cried, and a sunny glow of merriment came into her face, as though she had just been waiting for the Fiddler's nose to push the clouds aside.

Sali looked at her and saw her amusement. But she had already forgotten what caused it, and was now smiling at Sali for his sake alone. Astonished and confused, he gazed open-mouthed into her eyes, like a starving man who catches sight of a loaf of sweet, white bread, and cried:

"Oh, Vreeli, how lovely you are!"

Vrenchen smiled at him all the more happily and gave a low, attractive laugh whose musical ring sounded to poor Sali like the call of a nightingale.

"You witch!" he cried. "Where did you learn to laugh like that?"

"There's no witchcraft about it," said Vrenchen caressingly, taking his hand. "I had been longing to laugh like that. When I am on my own, I sometimes smile at odd things, but it is not the same thing. But as long as I am with you, I feel like laughing all the time. Do you care a little for me, too?"

"Oh, Vreeli," he cried, gazing devotedly into her eyes. "I have never looked at another girl. I always felt that it was you I would love some day, and you must have always been in my thoughts, even though I never knew it."

GOTTFRIED KELLER

"And you in mine – even more," Vrenchen broke in. "You had not seen me and did not know what I looked like, but I had often watched you from a distance, and sometimes even from quite close, without you knowing, so that I always knew what you looked like. Do you remember how often we used to come here as children? And the little cart? How small we were then, and how long ago it was! It makes us really old!"

"How old are you?" asked Sali, happy and delighted. "Seventeen?"

"Seventeen and a half," replied Vrenchen. "And how old are you? Wait, I know – you're about twenty."

"How do you know?"

"Never you mind!"

"Oh, go on!"

"No!"

"Oh, do tell me."

"No. I won't!"

"All right, we'll see!"

This childish exchange led Sali to lay his hands on her, pretending to make his clumsy caresses appear like a form of punishment. Playfully defending herself, she, too, allowed the conversation to go on, which, for all its childishness, they both found so charming and amusing.

Then Sali, his spirit roused, made bold to grasp her by the hands and draw her down among the poppies. She lay

50

there, looking up into the sun, her cheeks aglow and her lips parted, revealing two rows of shining white teeth. Her fine dark eyebrows met in the middle of her forehead, and her young breasts rose and fell as their hands, locked in confused embrace, pressed caressingly against her.

Sali's joy knew no bounds as he gazed at the beautiful slim form beside him. He knew that she was his, and he felt like a king.

"You've still got all your white teeth!" he smiled. "Do you remember how we used to count them? Have you learnt to count now?"

"They're not the same ones, you baby!" laughed Vrenchen. "The first ones came out long ago!"

Sali wanted to play their childish game again, but Vrenchen closed her ruby lips, sat up and began to plait a garland of poppies for her head. The broad ring of rich flowers gave the dark-skinned lass an irresistible charm, and what Sali held in his arms many would have paid dearly to have as a painting on their walls.

Then she sprang up and cried:

"My goodness, how hot it is! Here we are, sitting foolishly in the sun and getting burnt. Let's go and sit in the tall corn!"

Gently they slipped into the cornfield, leaving hardly a trace of the way they had come, and built themselves a little nook among the golden ears which stretched up above their heads, cutting off the outside world except for the deep blue sky. Clasped in each other's arms, they kissed each other until they grew weary – if weariness is the word to describe those glimpses of the transience of mortal life which come to lovers in their moments of ecstasy.

They listened to the larks singing high above and tried to seek them out with their keen eyes. When they thought they glimpsed one flashing across the sun like a meteor, they rewarded each other with a kiss, always trying to outdo each other and pretending to have seen one.

"Look! Up there!" Sali would whisper. And Vrenchen whispered back:

"I can hear it but I can't see it!"

"Up there, a little to the right of that white cloud."

And they would both stare at the heavens, their lips parted like the beaks of baby quails sitting in their nest, waiting only to press their lips together each time they imagined that they had seen another lark.

Suddenly Vrenchen drew away and said:

"So we agree that we both have a sweetheart, do we?"

"Yes," replied Sali, smiling; "it seems so."

"Are you fond of your sweetheart?" asked Vrenchen. "What does she look like? What can you tell me about her?"

"She is a lovely creature," said Sali, "with two brown eyes and ruby lips, and she walks on two legs. But I know as little about her mind as I do about the Pope of Rome! And what about yours?"

"He has two blue eyes and impudent lips, and he uses two strong, bold arms. But I know as little about his thoughts as I do about the Emperor of China!"

"We really know less about each other than if we had never met before," said Sali. "Time has made us strangers. What has been going on in that pretty little head of yours?"

"Oh, not much! All sorts of pranks occurred to me, but I was so depressed that I never carried them out."

"You poor darling!" cried Sali. "But you've learnt a trick or two by this time, I don't doubt!"

"If you really love me, you'll find out."

"When you are my wife, you mean?"

This last word made her tremble, and she held him tighter, kissing him tenderly again and again. Tears sprang to her eyes, and suddenly they both became sad as they thought of their parents' feud and of how little the future held for them.

"I must go now," she said with a sigh.

They got up, and were walking out of the cornfield when they saw Vrechen's father ahead of them. From the moment he had met Sali in the village he had been brooding suspiciously, with a petty curiosity born of idleness, on what the lad could have been up to. Then he had recalled the incident of the previous day. His malice and lurking hatred set his thoughts in motion, and soon his suspicions assumed definite shape. So although he had already reached the middle of the town, he turned round and trudged back to the village again.

When he reached the house, his daughter was nowhere to be seen. Hastening out on to the field, he caught sight of the basket in which she collected the vegetables; but Vrenchen herself was not in sight, and he was scanning his neighbour's cornfield for her when the frightened children emerged.

They stood there petrified. At first Marti, too, his face an ashen grey, stood looking at them angrily. Then he broke out in a fury and made to grasp Sali by the throat. The boy evaded him and darted away, but jumped forward again when he saw Marti seize the trembling girl savagely, give her a cuff on the head which sent her red garland flying, and take hold of her hair to drag her away and beat her.

Without thinking, Sali picked up a stone, and half in rage, half in fear of what might happen to Vrenchen, brought it down on Marti's head. The old man staggered about for a moment, then sank unconscious on to the stones, dragging the screaming Vrenchen with him.

Sali released her hair from his grasp and helped her to her feet, then stood there like a statue, helpless and terrified.

Looking down at the motionless body, Vrenchen shuddered and clutched her pale face with her hands.

"Have you killed him?" she whispered.

Sali nodded dumbly.

"Oh, God! My father! My poor father!" she cried frantically, throwing herself on to his body and raising his head, on which there was no sign of blood.

She let it sink down again. Sali knelt on the other side, and together, in deathly silence, their hands hanging limply and nervelessly at their sides, they stared at the lifeless features. At last Sali broke the silence.

"Perhaps he's not really dead!"

Vrenchen pulled a petal from a corn poppy and laid it on his pale lips. It stirred a little.

"He's still breathing!" she cried. "Run to the village for help!"

As Sali jumped up and was about to run off, she stretched out her hand and beckoned him back.

"Don't come back here," she said, "and don't say a word about how it happened. Nobody shall ever make me tell anything either."

Tears streamed down her face as she looked towards the poor, helpless Sali.

"Kiss me once more!" she cried. "But no! Leave now! It is all over – over for ever! We can never marry!"

She pushed him away, and he ran blindly towards the village. On his way he met a little boy who did not know him.

He told him to fetch the people nearest at hand, and described to him in detail where to take them. He then wandered off into the woods and spent the whole night roaming about there distractedly.

When morning came, he ventured out into the fields to see what had happened, and overheard from the conversation of some early passers-by that Marti was alive but unconscious, and that nobody knew, strangely enough, what had happened. On hearing this, Sali returned to the town and took refuge in the gloom and misery of his father's house.

Vrenchen kept her word. When questioned, she said only that she had found her father lying there in that state; and as he began to move and breathe more freely the next day, it was assumed that he had been drunk and struck his head on the stones, and there the matter ended. Vrenchen nursed him alone, only leaving his side to fetch medicaments from the doctor or to make herself something to eat, such as a plain soup of some kind. She lived on almost nothing, though she was awake day and night, and nobody helped her.

It was nearly six weeks before Marti regained consciousness, though he had already begun to take nourishment again and to show signs of life. But it was not the consciousness that he had known before. For as the power of speech returned to him, it became apparent that he had lost his reason. Only dimly did he recollect the past, and then as something amusing which was no real concern of his. He laughed idiotically and was for ever in high spirits; he lay in bed and poured forth all manner of incoherent thoughts and phrases, made grotesque grimaces, pulled his black woollen cap over his eyes and then down over his face, making his nose look like a coffin enveloped in a shroud.

Pale and anguish-stricken, Vrenchen listened to him patiently, shedding more tears over his present derangement than she had over his former cruelty. But when he did something particularly bizarre, she could not help laughing in spite of her grief, for her natural high spirits, now weighed down, were always ready to spring up again like a taut bow string, only to sink back into an even profounder sense of despair. After he was able to get up, it was impossible to do anything with him at all; he behaved like a child, rummaging around the house and laughing, or sitting in the sun, poking his tongue out and making long speeches to the beans.

It was at this same time that what little remained of his property was finally disposed of, for the neglect and disorder had reached such a pitch that his house and his last field, which had both been mortgaged for some time, were now officially auctioned. The farmer who had bought Manz's two fields took advantage of Marti's sorry situation to settle once and for all the old argument over the piece of land with the stones on it. This was the *coup de grâce* for Marti, but in his deranged state he no longer understood anything of what was going on.

When the sale was over, the poor, demented Marti was sent to a public institution in the capital of the canton. The pitiful creature, who was in good health and always ready to eat, was given a good meal, then put in an ox cart and taken to the town by a poor farmer who was on his way to sell a few sacks of potatoes there. Vrenchen sat in the cart with her father on his ride to this place of living burial.

It was a sad and bitter journey, but Vrenchen watched over her father carefully and attended to his every need; even if his antics attracted attention, and people ran after the cart as it passed through the villages, she did not look about her or become restless. At last they reached the rambling old building in the town. Its courtyards, its bright gardens and its long corridors were full of poor creatures like Marti, all dressed in white smocks and wearing stout leather caps on their bony heads.

Vrenchen watched as he too was put into this uniform. He was as happy as a sandboy, and pranced about and sang.

"Good day to you, gentlemen!" he cried to his new companions. "What a splendid place you have here! Go back, Vreeli, and tell your mother that I shan't be coming home any more! I like it better here!"

I heard a hedgehog barking as he crawled into the fold!
O maiden, give your kisses to the young and not the old!
The Rhine and the Danube flow into the sea;
the dark-eyed maid yonder's the right one for me!

"Why don't you go, child? You look a picture of misery, and I am so happy!"

An attendant told him to be quiet and led him away to do some light work, while Vrenchen went back to the cart. Sitting down in it, she took out a piece of bread and began to eat. Then she fell asleep, and slept until the farmer came to drive back to the village.

It was dark by the time they arrived. Vrenchen went back to the house in which she had been born and in which she had only two more days to live. For the first time in her life she was completely alone. She lit the fire to warm up what was left of the coffee, and sat down by the hearth in utter desolation. She yearned to see Sali just once more, and tormented herself with this thought, but her grief and sadness made her yearning bitter, and this in turn only intensified her misery.

As she was sitting there, her head in her hands, a figure came in through the open door. She looked up.

"Sali!" she cried, throwing her arms round his neck. Then they looked at each other in alarm, and each cried in the same breath:

"But how miserable you look!"

And indeed, the one looked as pale and haggard as the other. Forgetting all that had happened, she drew him close to herself by the hearth and said:

"Have you been ill, or have things been bad with you too?"

"No, I am not ill," replied Sali. "I am only sick with longing for you. And there are some strange goings-on at home; my father has invited in a lot of suspicious-looking characters, and it looks to me as if he has taken to harbouring thieves. That is why our tavern is so full at the moment – until the whole affair comes to a terrible end. My mother is caught up in it as well, out of a greedy desire to see some money coming in; she thinks that she can put the whole disreputable business on a proper basis by trying to keep some order in the place. I had nothing to do with it, and besides, I just kept thinking of you day and night. All kinds of tramps come to our inn, so we heard every day what was happening in your family, and the news made my father as happy as a child. We were told that your father had been taken to the almshouse today. I knew you must be alone, so I came out to see you."

Vrenchen poured out all her troubles to him, yet with the ease of someone relating a series of joyful events, for she was so happy to have Sali with her. She even managed to produce a bowl of warm coffee which she made him share with her.

"But what will you do," said Sali, "if you have to leave this house the day after tomorrow?"

"I don't know," replied Vrenchen. "I suppose I shall have to go and work as a maid. I cannot bear to live without you, Sali, but you can never be mine, because it was you who struck the blow that made my father insane. We could never have the peace of mind to build a life on this foundation."

Sali gave a sigh.

"Many times," he said, "I was on the point of joining the army or looking for a job as a farmhand in some far-off district, but I cannot leave while you are still here. My unhappiness seems to make my love stronger and more unbearable, and my whole life is torn apart in the struggle."

Vrenchen smiled lovingly at him. They leant back against the wall, basking in the radiant glow which outshone their sadness and proclaimed their love. And soon, sitting on the hard stones, without pillow or cushion, they slept softly and peacefully, like children in a cradle.

Dawn was already breaking when Sali awoke. Gently he tried to rouse Vrenchen, but she nestled drowsily against him and would not be wakened. Then he kissed her passionately. Opening her eyes, she cried, gazing up at him:

"Oh Sali! I was dreaming of you! I dreamt that we were dressed in our finery and dancing at our wedding, hour after hour, blissfully happy and without a care in the world. We longed to kiss each other but something kept drawing us apart – and now I see that it was you who were disturbing us! O how wonderful that you are here!"

Throwing her arms round him, she kissed him again and again.

"And what did you dream about?" she asked him, stroking his cheek.

"I dreamt that I was walking down a never-ending lane in the forest, and that you were walking ahead of me in the distance; sometimes you looked round and smiled and beckoned me on – that was all. It was the happiest moment of my life!"

As they walked together to the door, they looked at each other and began to laugh, for Vrenchen's right cheek and Sali's left, which had lain against each other as they slept, were quite red, while the other two had been made even paler than usual by the coolness of the night air. Gently they rubbed their two cold, pale cheeks together to make them as red as the others. The crisp morning air, the freshness of the dew and the tranquillity of the dawning day made them joyful and oblivious to their cares. Vrenchen in particular seemed filled with a spirit of carefree gaiety.

"Tomorrow evening," she said, "I shall have to leave this house and find shelter elsewhere. But before then I want to enjoy one real moment of happiness – with you. I want to dance and dance with you in my joy, for I cannot lose the vision of how we danced in my dream."

"But I want to know where you are going to live," said Sali. "And I want us to dance as well, my darling. Yet where can we go?"

"Tomorrow there are two fairs not far from here," answered Vrenchen. "People will not know us there or take much notice of us. I will wait for you by the lake. Then we can go where we want and enjoy ourselves – just for this once! But," she then added sadly, "we have no money, so it is no use."

"Leave that to me," said Sali. "I'll get some."

"But not from your father. Not that stolen money!"

"No, no! I still have my silver watch; I'll sell that."

"I would not have you change your mind," said Vrenchen, blushing. "If we could not dance tomorrow, I think I would die!"

"It would be best if we could both die!" murmured Sali.

They parted with a sad embrace, smiling lovingly at each other as they thought of the following day.

"When will you come?" Vrenchen cried after him.

"At eleven o'clock, at the latest!" he called back. "We'll eat lunch together in style!"

"Oh, yes!" she exclaimed eagerly. "Then come at half-past ten instead!"

He had almost gone when she called him back again, with a look of sudden dejection on her face.

"We cannot go!" she cried through her tears, "I have no Sunday shoes left. I even had to wear these old clogs to go into town yesterday!"

Sali was taken aback.

"No shoes?" he said. "Then you must wear your clogs."

"But I can't dance in these!"

"Then we shall have to buy some."

"But how can we?"

"There are plenty of shoe shops in Seldwyla, and in less than two hours I shall have the money."

"But we can't walk around together in Seldwyla. And besides, there won't be enough money to buy shoes as well."

"We shall have to make it enough! I will buy the shoes and bring them with me tomorrow."

"Don't be silly! They wouldn't fit!"

"Then give me one of your old ones. No, wait a moment. I have a better idea. I'll measure your foot – that's easily done."

"All right. I'll find a piece of string."

She sat down again on the hearth, pulled up her skirt a little and slipped off one of her clogs, uncovering the white stockings she had been wearing since her journey the previous day. Sali knelt down and measured her foot as well as he could, taking its length and breadth, and carefully knotting the string to mark the size.

"Why, you're almost as good as a shoemaker!" she laughed, blushing and looking down at him affectionately. Sali reddened too and held her foot longer than he need have done. Drawing it away with an even deeper blush, she embraced the embarrassed Sali again, kissed him impulsively and then told him to go.

As soon as he reached the town, he took his watch to a jeweller, who gave him between six and seven florins for it, and a few more for the silver chain. He now felt rich, for never before had he had so much money in his possession. If only today were over and Sunday already here, he thought to himself, so that he could buy the happiness that he wanted that day to bring; and the sinister shadow of the future only added a strange lustre to the longed-for pleasures of the morrow.

The rest of the day he spent in looking for a pair of shoes for Vrenchen. It was the most delightful task he had ever undertaken. He went from one shop to another asking to see all the ladies' shoes they had, until he finally decided on a dainty pair far prettier than Vrenchen had ever worn. He hid them under his jacket and did not let go of them for a single moment during the rest of the day. He even took them to bed with him and put them under his pillow.

As he had been with Vrenchen that morning, and knew that he would see her again the next day, he slept soundly and peacefully. When dawn came, he rose happily and began to brush and clean his shabby Sunday clothes as best he could.

His mother, noticing this in surprise, asked him where he was going, for he had not taken such care over his appearance for many a day. Sali replied that he wanted to go out and see something of the world: it would ruin his health to have to stay in the house all the time.

"What sort of life is that," grumbled his father, "wandering about aimlessly?"

"Let the boy go," retorted his mother. "It may do him good. Just look what a picture of misery he is!"

"Have you got any money?" asked Manz. "And if so, where did you get it?"

"I don't need any," answered Sali.

"Here's a florin," said his father, throwing it across to him. "Go and spend it in the inn, so that people don't think we're hard up."

"I'm not going to the village, so you can keep the money!"

"It would be wasted on you anyway, you pig-headed fool!" cried Manz, thrusting the florin back into his pocket.

But Sali's mother, who did not know why she should feel so despondent and so concerned about her son that morning, gave him a large black neckerchief with a red border which she had hardly ever worn but which the boy had always wanted. He wound it round his neck and let the long ends hang down; then, for the first time in his life, instead of turning his collar down, he turned it right up to his ears like a man of the world. So, shortly after seven o'clock, he set out in manly pride, carrying Vrenchen's shoes in the inner pocket of his jacket.

At that moment he felt a strange urge to stretch out his hand to his father and mother as he left, and when he was out on the road he looked back at the house once more.

"Do you know what I think?" said Manz. "He's chasing after some girl or other. That would be the last straw!"

"Perhaps he will find happiness with her," said his wife. "If he did, it would be wonderful for the poor boy."

"Oh, wonderful," sneered Manz. "If he has the misfortune to get hold of the sort of chatterbox I've got, it will certainly be wonderful for the poor wretch!"

At first Sali made for the river, where he had arranged to meet Vrenchen, but on the way he changed his mind and went straight to her house, for he felt he could not wait till the appointed hour. "Why worry what people will say?" he thought to himself. "I'm an upright fellow and afraid of no one. Besides, nobody has ever lifted a finger to help us."

So without further ado he opened Vrenchen's door. To his surprise he found her sitting there fully dressed in her finest clothes, waiting only for her shoes. When he saw her, he stopped in his tracks and stared at her open-mouthed, so lovely did she look. Her slim form was sheathed in a simple blue cotton dress, fresh and fragrant, and round her neck she wore a kerchief of snow-white muslin. Her brown locks, usually so dishevelled, were neatly combed. She had scarcely been outside the house for weeks, and her complexion had become even paler than before, as though from sorrow. But this pallor now gave way to the flush of love and joy, and on her dress she wore a beautiful spray of rosemary, asters and roses.

She had been sitting by the open window, revelling in the fresh, sunlit morning air. When she caught sight of Sali, she stretched out her soft, bare arms towards him and cried:

"How happy I am that you have come so early! Have you really brought the shoes? I shan't stand up until I've got them on!"

He took the cherished present from his pocket and gave it to her. She kicked off her old clogs and eagerly slipped into the new ones. They fitted perfectly. She got up from her chair to see how they felt, and walked delightedly up and down a few times. Then she drew her long blue dress up a little and looked admiringly at the red woollen bows which graced the new shoes, while Sali could nor take his eyes off the charming figure tripping joyfully and excitedly to and fro.

"Are you looking at my posy?" she said. "Isn't it pretty? They were the last flowers I could find in the wilderness outside. There was a rose growing in one place, and an aster in another; and now that they're tied together, nobody could ever tell that they came from such a barren waste. So now that there is not a flower left, and the house is empty, it is time for me to leave."

Sali looked round and noticed for the first time that all the furniture had gone.

"Poor Vreeli." he murmured. "Have they taken every-thing?"

"Yesterday they took everything they could," she replied, "and did not even want to leave me my bed. But now I've sold that too and got some money of my own. Look!"

And she took a few shining talers from the pocket of her dress and showed them round him.

"The man from the orphanage who was here," she went on, "told me to take them and start looking for a job in the town straight away."

"But there is not a single thing left," said Sali, who had looked into the kitchen, "not a stick of wood, not a saucepan, not a single knife. Did you not have any breakfast?"

"No," answered Vrenchen. "I could have fetched something but then I thought it would be better to stay hungry so that I could eat a big meal when we go out together. How happy I am going to be today!"

"And how happy I would be if I could only touch you, you lovely creature!" cried Sali.

"You would only spoil my dress! And if we can spare my little posy for a while, it will make up for the way you ruffle my hair."

"Let's be on our way, then!"

"No, we must wait until they come to fetch the bed. When they have left, I shall shut the door on the empty house and never come back. The woman who bought the bed can look after my few things."

They sat down opposite each other and waited.

The woman soon arrived, a buxom matron with a loud voice; with her came a lad who was to carry the bedstead. When she saw Vrenchen sitting there in her finery, she gaped at the couple wide-eyed, planted her hands on her hips and exclaimed:

"Well, well, Vreeli! You're doing things in grand style – dressed like a princess, and with a friend, too!"

"You're right!" replied Vrenchen with a smile. "And do you know who he is?"

"He looks to me like Sali Manz. 'East and West shall never meet', says the proverb – but with people it's different! Yet take heed, child, and remember what happened to your fathers."

"Oh, all that belongs to the past," answered the smiling

Vrenchen in a friendly, almost condescending tone. "You see, Sali is my fiancé."

"Your fiancé? Well, well!"

"Yes, and he is a rich man, too. He has just won a hundred thousand florins in the sweepstake. Just think of that!"

"A hundred thousand florins!" cried the woman, giving a violent start and clapping her hands together in amazement.

"A hundred thousand florins!" repeated Vrenchen gravely.

"Heavens above! I don't believe you, child. You're telling tales!"

"You can believe what you like!"

"But even if it is true, and you do marry him, what will you do with the money? Are you really going to live like a lady of rank?"

"Of course I am! The wedding will be in three weeks!"

"You're making it all up, you deceitful girl!"

"He has already bought a magnificent house in Seldwyla with a big garden and a vineyard. You must come and visit us when we have settled in!"

"What stories you do tell!"

"You'll see how beautiful it is. I'll make you some fine coffee and offer you sweet rolls with butter and honey."

"Then I'll certainly come!" cried the woman, her eyes glinting greedily and her mouth watering.

"And if you come at midday on your way back from the market, there will be some strong broth and a glass of wine waiting for you!"

"That's just what I would like!"

"And I shan't forget to give you some crisp rolls and other titbits for your children."

"I can hardly wait!"

"If you have an hour to spare, you can rummage through my chest and cases. You are sure to find a pretty neckerchief, or a piece of silk, or a bright ribbon to decorate your skirt, or a piece of material for a new apron."

The woman danced with delight, swinging her skirts round and round.

"And if your husband needs money to buy a piece of land or some cattle, you know where to come. My dear Sali will always be pleased to invest his money profitably, and I am sure to have my own private fund for helping my intimate friends."

The woman was by now completely won over, and said affectionately:

"I always said that you were a good, kind girl! The Lord bless you for your generosity!"

"But in return I want you to be kind to me."

"Of course I will!"

"And to offer all your produce, whether it be fruit, potatoes or vegetables, first to me before you go to market, so that I can be sure of having a farmer I can rely on. I shall pay you as much as the others – you know that. There is nothing finer than a true friendship between a rich townswoman in her lonely villa and an upright countrywoman versed in the practical affairs of life. Many are the times when one welcomes such a friendship – in joy and suffering, at christenings and weddings, when the children go to school and are confirmed, when they embark on their apprenticeship and leave home, and in times of drought and flood, fire and hailstorm – from which God preserve us!"

"May God preserve us!" sobbed the woman, drying her eyes with her apron. "How wise and understanding you are! Happiness will surely come your way, or there is no justice in the world! You are beautiful and intelligent, and gifted in all manner of ways. I know no finer or nobler person anywhere, and the man that wins you will feel that he is living in paradise. If he doesn't, I'll give the rogue a piece of my mind! Do you hear what I say, Sali? Be nice to my Vreeli, or I'll teach you a lesson – lucky fellow that you are, to win such a prize!"

"Then take this bundle you promised to keep until I send for it – I may even come in my carriage to collect it in person, if you have no objection. I'll bring an almond cake with me, and you're sure to offer me a jug of milk in return."

"Lord have mercy! Give me the bundle!"

Vrenchen took the long sack into which she had stuffed her worthless possessions, and put it on top of the rolled-up mattress which the woman was already balancing on her head, so that it looked like a tottering pillar.

"It's almost too heavy," she said. "Can I come back for the rest?"

"No, no," said Vrenchen hastily, "we must leave at once, for we have a long journey ahead of us. We have got to visit some fine relations who have suddenly appeared on the scene since we have become rich. You know what people are."

"I do, indeed! God bless you – and think of me sometimes in your prosperity."

Keeping her balance with difficulty, the bundle on her head, she left, followed by the lad carrying Vrenchen's once brightly painted bed; the top, with its pattern of faded stars, he rested on his head, grasping the finely carved front posts like a Samson. Vrenchen leant against Sali and watched the procession go on its way. Catching a last glimpse of it as it passed by the garden, looking like a moving temple, she said:

"That would make a nice little chalet or pavilion if we put it in a garden with a little table and a bench, and planted convolvuluses around it. Would you sit there with me, Sali?"

"Yes, Vreeli, especially when the convolvulus had grown tall!"

"What are we waiting for? There is nothing more to keep us here. Let us lock the house and go!"

"Who will keep the key?"

Vrenchen looked around her.

"We'll hang it on the old halberd. Father often used to say that it had been in the house for over a hundred years, and now it's standing guard like the last sentry!"

They hung a rusty house key on a protruding piece of the rusty old weapon round which the beanstalks were twined, and left. Vrenchen went a little pale and held her hand to her eyes, and Sali had to lead her a little way. But she did not look back.

"Where shall we go first?" she asked.

"Let's walk out into the country," answered Sali, "where we can be happy all day. We have no need to hurry. Then towards evening we'll find somewhere to dance."

"So we can be together the whole day and go wherever we like!" cried Vrenchen. "...But I'm beginning to feel faint. Let's go first and have breakfast in some other village."

"All right," said Sali, "we'll get out of this place as quickly as we can."

Soon they were in open country, walking side by side through the meadows. It was a beautiful Sunday morning in September, not a cloud in the sky, and a soft haze hung over the hills and woods, giving the scene a solemn, mysterious atmosphere. The sound of church bells came from all quarters – on one side a deep, melodious chime from a rich village, on another two tinkling little bells from a poor parish. The lovers, resplendent in their finest clothes, did not think of what the end of the day would bring but surrendered themselves to the silent joy of the moment, roaming freely in the sunshine like a couple who were made for each other. Every sound or call that was heard in the stillness of that Sunday morning echoed in their souls, for love is like a bell which vibrates to the faintest, most distant sound and gives out its own special music.

Although they were hungry, the half-hour's walk to the next village seemed only a stone's throw, and shyly they entered the first inn they came to.

Sali ordered a large breakfast, and while it was being prepared, they sat quietly and watched the comings and goings in the light and roomy parlour.

The landlord was also a baker, and the pleasant smell of fresh-baked bread filled the whole house; baskets full of all kinds of bread were brought in, for after church the villagers used to come here to collect their white loaves or have their morning drink. The landlord's wife, a fine, handsome woman, was quietly and smilingly dressing her children, and when one of the little girls was ready, she ran across to Vrenchen, showed her how beautiful she looked and confided to her all her proud and happy secrets.

When the coffee was brought, strong and with a fine aroma, the young couple took their places hesitantly at the table, as though they were guests of the house. Soon, however, they began to feel more confident, and to whisper softly and happily to each other. Vrenchen was in raptures over the rich coffee, the thick cream, the warm rolls, the fresh butter and honey, the pancakes and all the other delicacies.

But her greatest joy came from seeing Sali beside her, and she ate with the eagerness of one who had been fasting for a whole year. The fine china and the silver coffee spoons, too, filled her with delight. The landlord's wife obviously considered them to be honest young folk who deserved to be treated with respect, and from time to time she sat down at their table and chatted to them, taking pleasure in their sympathetic conversation.

Vrenchen was so enchanted that she did not know whether she would rather go out into the countryside to roam with her sweetheart through the woods and meadows, or stay in the friendly inn so as to preserve the illusion, at least for a few hours, that the fine house was really hers. But Sali made the decision for her by declaring firmly that they had better be on their way, giving the impression that they had an important journey to make. The landlord and his wife accompanied them to the door, and although their poverty could not be disguised, they had displayed a perfect demeanour, and the host bade them a friendly farewell.

Courteously the young couple took their leave and walked out into the sunshine. Lost in dreams, and with no thought of their family strife and misery, they wandered side by side through the thick oak woods like the children of good, honourable parents. Vrenchen walked demurely along the damp, slippery path, her head bowed, her hands folded gracefully in front of her; Sali, however, held himself erect and stepped out boldly and purposefully, his eyes fixed on the trees around him like a woodman deciding which ones could most profitably be felled.

At last they awoke from their daydreaming, looked at each other and, seeing that they both still wore the same expression as when they left the inn, went red and hung their heads in embarrassment. But youth is carefree; the woods were green, the sky was blue – they were alone together again, and happiness returned to them once more.

But they did not remain alone for long, for the road began to fill with young couples and cheerful groups of friends, jesting and singing on their way home from church. Country folk have their favourite walks just like townspeople, but the parks where country folk go cost nothing to maintain, and are more beautiful as well. The countryman does not walk through his flowering fields with a special "Sunday-morning" mentality but strolls along lonely paths through copses and by green hilltops, resting by the verge of the forest or at the top of a grassy slope from which he can look out over the surrounding countryside, singing cheerfully and absorbing the unspoilt beauties of nature as he goes.

And since he does not do this as a penance but as a pleasure, he must have a feeling for nature which goes far beyond considerations of practical value, just like the old women who seek the paths along which they wandered as children, so young boys break off green twigs as they go. Even a rugged farmer in the prime of life takes delight in cutting a cane when his way takes him through the woods, paring off the leaves until only a green tuft is left at the top: bearing it aloft like a sceptre, he takes it with him into whatever office he visits, stands it solemnly in a corner, and invariably remembers to collect it again when he leaves, however serious his business has been; he carries it home in perfect condition and gives it to his youngest son, who is the only one permitted to break it.

When Sali and Vrenchen saw the strangers coming, they smiled to themselves and rejoiced in the thought that they, too, formed a couple. They left the road and slipped into the wood, following narrow lanes that led into silence and solitude, stopping where their fancy took them, then running off again. Their minds were as unclouded as the sky above them; they were oblivious to where they had come from and where they were going.

For all their excitement and their running to and fro, Vrenchen still looked as fresh and charming as in the early morning, while Sali had acted, not like a country bumpkin of twenty, the son of a dissolute tavern-keeper, but like a youth of good family, and there was something almost comic in the tenderness, the care and the reverence which he lavished on his radiant companion. For on this, the one day granted to them, they had to live through all the moods of love, to capture the lost serenity of days gone by, and to fill the moments that were left to them before the hour of their final sacrifice.

As they walked, they grew hungry again. Then from the top of a shady hill they saw a village nestling below in the sunshine, and decided to have lunch there. They hastened down the hill and entered the village, walking with the same modest air as when they had left the previous village. There was nobody to recognize them. Vrenchen in particular had hardly mixed with people at all in recent years, still less had she been to other villages. They thus passed for a pleasant, respectable young couple out for a walk.

They stopped at the first inn, and Sali ordered a substantial meal. A special table was decked for them, and as they sat there quietly and unassumingly, they looked at the fine walnut panelling, the walnut dresser, simple but well-polished, and the snow-white curtains.

The landlord's wife came up to them in a friendly manner and put a vase of fresh flowers on the table.

"You can feast your eyes on these till the soup comes!" she said with a smile. "And if I might make so bold as to ask – are you not a young couple on your way to the town to get married?"

Vrenchen blushed and was too embarrassed to raise her eyes. Sali kept silent too, and the woman continued:

"Well, you're both still young! Youthful wed eats happy bread, as the saying goes; and you are an attractive and honest-looking pair, so you need not be ashamed. A decent couple can make a success of life if they start young, and work hard, and are faithful to each other – and *that* you must certainly be, for you have many years before you. If you husband them well, they can be happy years. But don't mind me, young people. It's just that I was so pleased to see such a handsome couple."

The maidservant brought the soup, and as she had over-heard part of the conversation and had always hoped to get married herself, she looked jealously at Vrenchen, envious of the happiness that seemed to be in store for her. Back in the serving room she gave vent to her ill temper.

"They are another of those vagabond couples without a penny to their name," she said to the landlord's wife in a voice loud enough for all to hear; "they have no friends, no dowry, nothing but the prospect of poverty and beggary, yet they rush into the town to celebrate their wedding! Where shall we be if young things like that get married, when they can't even tie their own apron strings or make a proper soup? I'm really sorry for the boy – he's come to a pretty pass with his young Dulcinea!"

"Hold your tongue, you spiteful hussy!" hissed the wife. "I am not going to see any harm come to them. They seem a perfectly decent couple from the hills – they're probably mill-hands. Their clothes are shabby but clean, and as long as they love each other and work hard, they will go further than you with your malicious gossip. If you can't control your tongue, nobody is likely to propose to you – you surly creature!"

Thus Vrenchen experienced all that befalls a bride going to her wedding: the sympathy of an understanding woman; the jealousy of an old maid who both praises and pities the bridegroom out of personal spite, because she herself dearly wants to marry; and a delicious repast at the side of the bridegroom himself. Her cheeks bore the flush of a red carnation and her heart was thumping, but she ate and drank with enthusiasm and continued to be polite to the maidservant, though she could not resist casting affectionate glances at Sali and whispering to him, which only made the poor youth more embarrassed.

For a long time they sat there happily, as though reluctant to break the blissful spell. The innkeeper's wife brought them some pastries for dessert, and Sali ordered a stronger wine to go with them, which sent Vrenchen's blood coursing through her veins; she took only occasional sips, however, and sat there shyly and demurely, like a real bride. She played this role partly out of a roguish desire to see whether she really could act the part, and partly because she truly felt like a bride. As she sat there, held in the grip of both love and fear, the walls of the room seemed to close in on her, and she made Sali take her out into the open air again.

Instinctively they seemed to avoid returning to the side lanes where they would be alone, and silently they walked along the road, past the groups of people standing there, looking to neither left nor right.

When they had left the last house behind them and were on the way to the next village, in which the fair was being held, Vrenchen caught Sali's arm and said in a trembling whisper:

"Sali, why should we not give ourselves to each other and be happy?"

"I do not know why," he stammered, gazing at the soft September sunshine which covered the meadows, and struggling to control his emotions. They stopped to kiss each other, but a party of young folk came into view, and they parted and walked on.

The big village was already swarming with activity. The sound of festive music came from the stately inn, and the young villagers had started to dance, while in the square a few stalls had been set up, with pastries and sweets and cheap trinkets. The children were crowding around, together with others who had come rather to look than to buy.

Sali and Vrenchen went over to look as well, each with the wish to buy something for the other, since this was the first time that they had been to a fair together. Sali bought a big gingerbread house covered in gleaming white icing, with white doves sitting on its green roof and a little Cupid peeping out of the chimney, pretending to be a sweep; chubby-cheeked figures embraced each other at the open windows, their tiny red lips joined in a real kiss, since the painter had in his haste made only a single red daub for their two mouths. Their eyes were little black spots, and on the red door were inscribed the following lines:

"Come into my house, my darling!
Yet know, my dearest friend
That kisses are the currency
That people here must spend."

The maiden spake: "My hero,
I have no trace of fear!

My only thought is of the joys
That we can savour here!

And this it was that drew me,
To seek here thy embrace!"
So come, good lovers, follow now
The custom of this place!

Painted on the walls of the house, to the left and right of the door, were a gentleman in a blue cloak and a fine lady with a very large bosom, and in the spirit of the poem each was inviting the other inside.

For Sali, Vrenchen bought a heart, on one side of which was a slip of paper with the words:

An almond sweet is buried in this heart so gay and free;
But sweeter than the almond is the love I bear to thee!

On the other side was the inscription:

And when this heart is eaten, recall the words I say:
My love will live unsullied until the Judgement Day!

Eagerly they read these mottoes, and never did a poem strike so deep, or was adjudged so beautiful, as was this gingerbread doggerel. It seemed to have been written especially for them, so exactly did it mirror their own feelings.

"You have given me a home," said Vrenchen with a sigh. "And I have given you one, too – a true one. For our hearts are now our home, and we are carrying it about with us like the snails!"

"Then we are like two snails carrying each other's home!" smiled Sali.

"All the more reason why we should stay close together, so that each can be near his own!"

Not realizing that their jests were of the same kind as those of the many gingerbread shapes laid out before them, they continued to examine the sentimental inscriptions, particularly those attached to the lavishly decorated hearts, large and small, that lay there. Vrenchen discovered a gilt heart strung like a lyre, on which was written:

Soft music in this heart abounds;
The more you play it, the more it sounds!

And when she read this, she seemed to hear the sound of music in her own heart.

Then they found a portrait of Napoleon which bore the following motto:

Napoleon was a hero real,
With heart of oak and sword of steel.
My love is fair and fancy free,
Yet faithful she will ever be!

While pretending to be absorbed in reading such verses, they each made secret purchases: Sali bought a gilt ring with a green stone, and Vrenchen chose a black chamois ring crowned with a golden forget-me-not. They both seemed to be urged by the thought to give each other some little trinket when the hour of their parting came. So engrossed were they in what they were doing that they did not notice the people gradually gathering round them in curiosity. A number of girls and lads from their own village were there and formed a circle round them, struck by their Sunday clothes, but the young couple seemed totally oblivious to the outside world.

"Just look!" said a voice. "It's Vrenchen Marti with that young Sali from the town! See how attached they are to each other, how affectionate and devoted! I wonder where they're going?"

The bystanders' surprise sprang from a strange mixture of pity, contempt for the baseness and depravity of their parents, and envy of the young couple's happiness; for the pure love which they cherished for each other set them as far apart from the common mass as had their former loneliness and poverty.

Awaking at last from their reveries, they looked round them and saw the staring faces. No one greeted them, nor did they know whether they should greet the others – though this unfriendliness and mutual distrust were more the product of their embarrassment than a feeling of deliberate hostility.

Poor Vrenchen trembled and turned pale, but Sali led her away, and holding her little house in her hand, she followed him, although the cheerful sound of the band was coming from the inn and she longed so much to dance.

"We cannot dance here," said Sali, when they had moved some distance away.

"Then let us give up our plans, and I will try to find somewhere to stay for the night."

"No!" cried Sali. "You shall have your dance! That's why I bought the shoes! Let's go and join the poor folk; that's where we really belong, and they won't look down on us there. People always dance in the Garden of Paradise when the fair is here, because it belongs to the same parish, so let's go there. They might even give you a bed."

Vrenchen shuddered at the thought of sleeping for the first time in a strange place but involuntarily she followed her guide, who was now all she had in the world.

The Garden of Paradise was an inn beautifully set on a lonely hillside, with a wide view of the surrounding country, but it was only frequented by the lower classes, children of poor farmers and labourers, and all kinds of vagabonds. It had been built a hundred years ago by a rich eccentric as a small country house, but after he died, nobody wanted to live there. Since it could not be put to any useful purpose, the whole estate fell into decay and finally passed into the hands of a man who turned it into an inn. The appearance of the place, however, together with its name, remained unchanged.

It consisted of a single-storeyed building with a terrace on the roof, the sides of which were open and the roof supported by four weather-beaten sandstone pillars, one at each corner, depicting the four archangels. The portico was adorned with little cherubs, also carved in sandstone, with big heads and fat bodies, playing triangles, fiddles, pipes, cymbals and tambourines. These instruments had originally been painted gold, and the ceiling inside, as well as the outer walls of the whole building, were covered with faded frescoes depicting merry groups of angels and figures of singing, dancing saints. But everything was pale and blurred as in a dream, and vines now covered the whole surface, with dark grapes ripening in the midst of the thick foliage. The house was surrounded by large, untended chestnut trees, and gnarled rose trees sprawled over the ground like elderberry bushes.

The terrace was used for dancing, and from a long way off Sali and Vrenchen could see the figures up there, while crowds of revellers drank and jostled each other round the house below. Vrenchen, who was still reverently carrying her gingerbread house, looked like one of those religious benefactresses in old pictures, who bear in their hands a model of the church or nunnery which they have founded. But the house that was in Vrenchen's mind would never be built.

When she heard the cheerful dance music, however, she forgot her sorrows and wanted nothing but to dance with Sali. Threading their way through the people sitting in front of the inn and in the parlour, poor, ragged folk from Seldwyla and surrounding places who were looking for a cheap day's entertainment, they climbed the stairs and began to dance a waltz, gazing silently into each other's eyes.

When the waltz had ended, they looked round them. Vrenchen's little house was crushed, and she was just preparing to cry, when she looked up to see the sinister figure of the Black Fiddler.

He was sitting perched on a bench on top of a table, and looked as black as ever, but this time he had stuck a sprig of green pine needles in his hat, while at his feet stood a bottle of red wine and a glass. Yet although he stamped his feet the whole time he was playing his fiddle, he never knocked the bottle or glass over, so that the whole performance was like a step-dance. By his side sat a handsome but sad-looking young man with a horn, and a hunchback with a double bass.

Sali, too, shrank from the sight of the Fiddler, who, however, greeted them cordially and cried:

"I knew I would play a tune for you to dance to some day! So enjoy yourselves, young lovers, and let us drink to one another!"

He held out the glass to Sali, who took it and drank his health. When the Fiddler saw how frightened Vrenchen looked, he tried to console her, and succeeded in making her smile at some of his good-natured jests. Slowly her cheerfulness returned, and they were glad to have a friend there; indeed, they almost felt as though they were under the Fiddler's special care and protection.

On and on they danced, forgetting both themselves and the world in the singing and rejoicing around them, that rang out far into the countryside as the silver haze of the autumn evening began to settle. They danced until darkness fell and most of the merry guests had dispersed to their distant homes, singing and shouting.

Those who stayed were the real fraternity of the road, who were set on following a joyful day with a joyful night. Among them were some motley-dressed characters who appeared to know the Fiddler well, such as a young lad in a green corduroy jacket and a crumpled straw hat round which he had twined a garland of mountain-ash leaves. This boy had with him a wild-looking girl in a cherry-red cotton skirt with white spots, who had set on her head a coronet of vines, with a cluster of grapes over each temple. This couple was the most abandoned of all those present, darting from one corner to another, and dancing and singing without pause.

A slim, attractive girl was also there, dressed in a faded black silk dress and with a white linen scarf on her head, the long point hanging down at the back; the red stripes woven into it showed that it had been a towel or a serviette. Beneath this head-covering glistened a pair of deep blue eyes. Round her neck and on her breast hung a necklace, not of coral but of six rows of mountain-ash berries threaded on a string. The whole evening she danced alone, invariably turning down the young men's offers. Lightly and gracefully she tripped round the room, smiling each time she passed the sad-looking horn player, who looked the other way whenever she approached. Other young women were also there with their consorts, all shabbily dressed but no less friendly and merry for that.

When darkness fell, the landlord refused to light the candles, claiming that the wind would only blow them out; besides, he said, the full moon would soon be up, and moonlight was quite sufficient illumination for the money that they had spent. This decision met with universal approval, and the company took up position on the parapet, watching the red glow that was already visible on the horizon.

As soon as the moon's rays fell on the open dance floor, the couples began to dance again, this time gently and in blissful happiness, as though they were dancing by the glow of a thousand candles. The strange light seemed to bring them closer together, and in the general merriment Sali and Vrenchen could not but join in and dance with other partners. Yet whenever they were drawn apart for a while, they quickly sought each other again and rejoiced as though they had not seen each other for years.

Whenever he had to dance with another girl, Sali looked depressed and ill-tempered, and kept looking round for Vrenchen. But she did not look at him as she swept past, and, her cheeks flushed like a rose, seemed happy to dance with any partner.

"Are you jealous, Sali?" she asked, when the musicians had become tired and stopped playing for a while.

"Heaven forbid!" he replied. "How could I be?"

"Then why do you look so cross when I dance with other boys?"

"It's not your dancing with other boys, but my having to dance with other girls! I feel as though I'm holding a piece of wood in my arms! Don't you feel the same way?"

"Oh, I'm always happy when I'm dancing, as long as I know that you are there too. But if you ever went away and left me alone, I think I would die!"

They went down the stairs and stood in front of the inn. Vrenchen threw her arms around him and clasped him to her slender, trembling body, laying her flushed, tear-stained cheek against his.

"We cannot stay together," she sobbed, "yet I cannot leave your side, even for a single moment."

Sali held her tightly in his arms and covered her with kisses. Desperately he tried to think of an answer but he could find none. For even had he been able to outlive the despair and unhappiness which attended his own life, his inexperience and his youthful passion ill equipped him to face a long time of trial and renunciation. And there also remained the figure of Vrenchen's father, whom he had rendered helpless for the rest of his life.

They both knew that they could only find true happiness by becoming man and wife. Lonely and abandoned as they were, this thought was the last flicker of that flame of honour which had burned in their families in times gone by, and which their ambitious fathers had extinguished when, thinking to augment this honour by adding to their material wealth, they had so recklessly laid hands on the property of another.

Such events happen every day, but from time to time fate decides to intervene, and brings together two such seekers after fame and riches, letting them provoke and finally devour each other like wild beasts. For it is not only kings and emperors who miscalculate this way: men from the humblest cottages can be equally guilty, showing through their erring ways that the obverse of a badge of honour is a badge of shame.

Sali and Vrenchen, however, remembered how their families had once enjoyed honour and esteem, and how they had been brought up as the children of trusted and respected fathers. Then they had been drawn apart, and when they finally came together again, they saw in each other that happiness which their families had lost, and their memories made them cling all the more passionately to each other; the happiness they craved had to have a firm foundation, and though their blood throbbed through their veins, urging them to consummate their union, that foundation seemed to be ever beyond their grasp.

"It's dark now," said Vrenchen, "and we must part."

"Do you think I will leave you here alone?" cried Sali. "No, never!"

"But it will be no easier when tomorrow comes."

"Let me give you a piece of advice, you young simpletons!" came a harsh voice from behind them – and the Fiddler stepped out of the shadows.

"There you stand," he went on, "wanting to be united but not knowing which way to turn. My advice is, take each other as you are and have done with it. Come into the mountains with me and my friends. You won't need a parson there, or money, or a licence, or honour, or a marriage bed – nothing but your own desires. Things are not at all bad where we live: the air is healthy, and there is plenty to eat if you are prepared to work. The green woods are our home, and there we live and love as we please; and in winter we either make ourselves a warm resting place or hide in the farmer's hay loft. So make up your minds! Call this your wedding day and come with us, then you'll be rid of all your troubles! You can live happily ever after – or anyway for as long as you have a mind to. People reach a ripe old age in the freedom which we enjoy, believe me! – And don't think," he continued, "that I bear you any ill-will for what your parents did to me. I won't deny that it gives me a certain satisfaction to see that you have come to this pass, but I am content to leave it at that. You are welcome to join us. And if you decide to do so, I will do my best to help you."

His manner became friendlier as he said this.

"Well, think it over for a while," he concluded, "but if you take my advice, you'll come along with us. Forget the world, be married and turn your back on the others! Think of the bridal chamber waiting for you in the depths of the forest – or in a haystack, if it's too cold!"

He went into the inn. Holding the trembling Vrenchen in his arms, Sali said:

"What shall we do? Why not let the world go its way, and love each other fully and freely?"

But he said it more as a despairing jest than in earnest, and Vrenchen, kissing him, replied with a childlike simplicity:

"No, that is not the way I want things to be. The young horn player and the girl in the silk dress took that way out, they say, and were deeply in love; last week she was unfaithful to him for the first time, but he could not get over it, and now he is sullen and refuses to speak either to her or to anyone else, and the others all laugh at him. As a form of mock penance she dances by herself and will not talk, thus ridiculing him still further. You can see from the poor boy's face that he will make it up with her before the day is out, but I do not want to live where things like this go on. I would give anything to call you mine, and I could not bear the thought of being unfaithful to you."

Her body quivered as she pressed herself against him. Ever since leaving the inn that afternoon, where the landlady had taken her for a young bride, the thought of nuptial bliss had burned within her, and the further the realization of this bliss receded, the more uncontrollable her desire became.

Sali, too, felt this desperate longing, for although he had no wish to follow the Fiddler's invitation, it had set his mind in a whirl. In a choking voice he said:

"Let's go inside and have something to eat and drink."

They entered the parlour, where the only people left were

the party of vagabonds, who were seated round a table, eating their humble repast.

"Here come the bride and groom!" cried the Fiddler. "Rejoice, young people, and plight your troth to each other!"

They allowed themselves to be led to the table, happy of a chance to be able to escape from themselves for a moment. Sali ordered wine and more food to be brought, and a merry party commenced. The sulky young horn player had made his peace with his unfaithful partner and was fondling her passionately; the other pair of lovers, too, sang and drank and caressed each other lovingly, while the Fiddler and the hunchback played away to their hearts' content.

Sali and Vrenchen sat there without speaking, clasped in each other's arms. Then suddenly the Fiddler called for order and performed a mock ceremony which was meant to represent a wedding. He made them take each other's hands, then bade the assembled company rise and come up one by one to congratulate the young couple and welcome them to the fraternity. They submitted in silence, taking it as a jest, but at the same time trembling in apprehension.

Roused by the strong wine, the little gathering became more and more excited and made more and more noise, until at last the Fiddler gave the order to depart.

"We have a long journey before us," he cried, "and it is already past midnight. Come! Let us escort the bride and bridegroom on their road! I will lead the way myself and set the pace!"

Their minds in a whirl, the poor young lovers did not know which way to turn, and helplessly allowed themselves to be put at the head of the procession. Behind them came the other two couples, and the hunchback brought up the rear, his instrument over his shoulder.

The Fiddler started off down the hillside, playing his violin like one possessed, and the others skipped along behind him, laughing and singing. On they went through the night, past silent fields and meadows and into Sali's and Vrenchen's own village, where all had long been steeping.

As they made their way through the quiet streets and past their homes, they were gripped by a feeling of wild abandon and danced along madly behind the Fiddler, kissing each other, laughing and weeping. They danced their way up the ridge where the three fields had lain, and when they reached the top, the Fiddler played in an even greater frenzy, leaping about like a demon and daring his companions to vie with him in his revelry. Even the hunchback joined in, groaning under the weight of his burden, and the whole hillside echoed as though with the noise of the Witches' Sabbath.

Holding Vrenchen tightly in his arms, Sali, who was the first to regain his senses, forced her to stand still; then, to stop her wild singing, he kissed her firmly on the lips. They stood there in silence, listening as the wedding revellers wended their noisy way across the field and disappeared into the distance along the river bank, without even noticing that the young lovers were no longer with them. The sound of the Fiddler's violin, the girls' laughter and the boys' shouts still rang out for a time into the night, until they too, died away and all was still.

"We have escaped from the others," said Sali, "but how can we escape from ourselves? How can we ever live apart?"

Vrenchen could find no answer. She clung to him, her breast heaving.

"Should we not go back to the village?" he said. "Perhaps someone there would take care of you. Then tomorrow you could be on your way again."

"Without you?"

"You must forget me."

"That I shall never do! Could you forget me?"

"That is not the point, my sweetheart," said Sali, stroking her flushed cheeks as she leant against him and tossed her head feverishly from side to side. "It is you I am thinking of. You are young, and things are bound to work out for you, wherever you are."

"And what about you, you old man?"

"Come!" said Sali impulsively, leading her away. After a few yards they stopped again and embraced each other. The silence of the world was music in their souls; the only sound came from the river flowing softly by.

"How beautiful it is everywhere! Can you hear something that sounds like singing and bells chiming?"

"It's the water rushing past. There's no other sound."

"But there is, listen! It's all around us!"

"It must be our own blood in our ears."

They listened for a while to the mysterious sounds, whether imagined or real, which issued from the great stillness around them, or which they confused with the magic effects of the moonlight that seemed to hover above the white autumn mist which covered the ground.

Suddenly Vrenchen remembered something, and searching in the bodice of her dress, she exclaimed:

"I bought a souvenir that I wanted to give you."

And taking the simple ring, she placed it on his finger.

Sali took out his own ring, put it on Vrenchen's hand and said:

"We both had the same thought."

Holding up her hand in the pale moonlight, Vrenchen examined her ring.

"Oh, how lovely it is!" she cried, smiling. "Now we are really betrothed – you are my husband and I am your wife! Just let's pretend it's really true for a minute – just until that wisp of cloud has passed across the moon, or until we have counted up to twelve. Kiss me twelve times."

GOTTFRIED KELLER

Sali's love was no less strong than Vrenchen's, but he had never felt that marriage held the inescapable decision between life and death. She, however, saw with passionate intensity either the one or the other possibility, each absolute and unconditional.

But now a new realization dawned on her, and the emotions of a young girl suddenly turned to the fierce desires of a woman. Sali's embraces became more and more urgent as he held her in his savage grip, covering her with kisses. Vrenchen felt this change in him, and a shudder went through her body, but before the cloud had passed across the face of the moon, she was seized by the same passion. As they caressed each other, their hands came together, and their two rings were joined in an involuntary and symbolic expression of their union.

His heart throbbing, Sali whispered breathlessly:

"There is only one way out for us, Vrenchen. This must be our wedding hour – then we must leave the world behind. Over there is the river – where no one can part us. We shall have given each other our love, whether for a single night or for a lifetime."

And Vrenchen answered:

"Sali, the same thought has been in my mind hundreds of times – that we should die together and put an end to everything. Promise me that we shall do so!"

"It is all that is left to us," said Sali, "for nothing but Death can take you from me now!"

Tears of joy came to her eyes. Then jumping up, she ran as lithe as a deer across the field and towards the river. Sali ran after her, for he thought she was trying to escape from him, while Vrenchen, for her part, thought that he wanted to hold her back. On they ran, one behind the other, and Vrenchen laughed like a runaway child. When they reached the river, they stopped and faced each other.

"Are you sad?"

"No, I'm happy."

Mindless of their sorrows, they descended the bank and ran along by the water's edge, overtaking the current in their eagerness to find a place to lie. Their one feeling now was of the ecstasy that bound them; the final parting that was to follow seemed but a triviality, and they thought as little about it as a wastrel thinks about the morrow when he has spent his last penny.

"My flowers shall show me the way!" cried Vrenchen. "Look, they are withered already!" And plucking the posy from her breast, she threw it into the water and sang:

"But sweeter than the almond is the love I bear to thee!"

"Stop!" cried Sali suddenly. "Here is your bridal bed!"

They had come to a path that led from the village down to the river. Here there was a landing stage to which a large boat, piled high with hay, was tied up. Feverishly Sali began to untie the mooring ropes. Taking hold of his arm, Vrenchen said with a smile:

"What are you doing? Do you mean to steal the farmers' hay barge?"

"This is their wedding-gift to us – a floating bridal chamber and a bed such as no bride has ever seen! Besides, they will find their property down by the weir, which is where they would take it in any case, and they will never know what happened. Look, it's rocking and wants to move out into the stream!"

The boat was lying in fairly deep water a few yards from the bank. Lifting Vrenchen high in the air, Sali carried her through the water towards the boat, but she hugged him so tightly, caressing him and squirming about in his arms like a fish, that he could hardly keep his footing in the strong current. She tried to dip her hands and face in the water, exclaiming:

"Let me touch the cool water too! Do you remember how cold and wet our hands were when we first gave them to each other? We were catching fish then; now we're going to become fish ourselves – two fine fat ones!"

"Be quiet, you little witch," said Sali, striving to keep his balance as he carried his struggling sweetheart through the water, "or we'll be swept away!"

He lifted her on to the boat and pulled himself up after her;

then he helped her to climb on to the sweet smelling hay and got up beside her. And as they sat there together, the boat drifted slowly out into the middle of the current and floated gently downstream.

The river wended its way through tall, dark woods which cast their shadow over the water, and through open country; sometimes it glided through peaceful villages, sometimes past lonely cottages. In parts of its course it flowed so slowly that it became like a tranquil lake, and the boat almost stopped; in other parts it surged past craggy rocks and left the sleeping banks quickly behind.

With the glow of dawn a town came into view, its steeples rising above the silver waters. The setting moon cast a shaft of light on to the surface of the water, and the boat drifted down the river along this gold-red path. As it approached the town, two pale figures rose in the chill of the September morning and slipped from the dark hulk into the cold waters below, clasped in each other's arms.

A short while afterwards the boat struck a bridge and lodged there, undamaged. The bodies were found later below the town, and when their identity had been established, the newspapers reported that a young couple belonging to two impoverished and degenerate families which had been locked in a bitter feud, had drowned themselves in the river after dancing happily the whole afternoon and enjoying themselves at a fair.

It was also assumed that there was a connection between this event and an incident in the same area involving a hay barge which had drifted downstream into the town with no one on board: it appeared that the couple had stolen the boat in order to celebrate their sinful union. And this, the writer added, could only be seen as just one more proof of the growing depravity and immorality of the times.

Notes

p. 6, *Bezirksrat*: A public body roughly corresponding to a local district council. [*Transl.*]

p. 13, *What he... knows*: A phrase taken from Heine. [*Transl.*]